Leslie

SPRINGSONG 🌺 BOOKS

Andrea   Kara

Anne   Kathy

Carrie   Leslie

Colleen   Lisa

Cynthia   Melissa

Erica   Michelle

Gillian   Paige

Jenny   Pamela

Jessica   Sara

Joanna   Sherri

Tiffany

Leslie

Jeanne Anders

BETHANY HOUSE PUBLISHERS
MINNEAPOLIS, MINNESOTA 55438

Leslie
SpringSong edition published 1996
Copyright © 1987
Joan Wester Anderson

Published by Bethany House Publishers
A Ministry of Bethany Fellowship, Inc.
11300 Hampshire Avenue South
Minneapolis, Minnesota 55438

Library of Congress Catalog Card Number 86-72892.

ISBN 1-55661-736-4

Printed in the United States of America

To all those who see Him in the tiny and vulnerable,
the homeless and afraid.

JEANNE ANDERS, a wife and mother of five, began her freelance writing career at her kitchen table in 1974. Since then she has published hundreds of magazine articles and many books, including an inspirational titled *The Language of the Heart* (Zondervan). Jeanne also enjoys a busy sideline as a speaker, discussing marriage and family topics with audiences around the country. She is active in her church Bible study and pro-life groups.

1

The small Volkswagen slowed down as Leslie turned off the expressway at the Cincinnati exit. Ahead of her loomed the city's crisp skyline, reflecting the glare of the setting sun. She had never been in this part of the country before, but Cincinnati was known as a cosmopolitan city, and would surely offer the help she sought. It was large enough to provide anonymity too; she had decided that on the long, steamy drive across Indiana. And finally—Leslie sighed wearily, pushing a strand of red-gold hair out of her eyes—she was just too hot and tired to drive any farther. Cincinnati would have to do.

Turning onto the cloverleaf, she glanced at the baby sleeping peacefully in the car seat next to her. A quick smile lit her drawn features. However irresponsible her sister Lee had been, she had at least given her infant daughter a fitting name. Even at four weeks old, Penny's copper-colored curls delicately ringed her little head, swirling damply against the tiny ears. Leslie noticed the baby's fist pressed tightly against her mouth, and smiled again. She had discovered Penny only a few days ago, but already she was beginning to love her.

Traffic slowed, and Leslie steered the car into the lane marked "Downtown Cincinnati." Common sense told her that a hospital or clinic would most likely be located in the center of a large city, and she needed to find a doctor as soon as possible. Little Penny might look sweet and contented, but Leslie's practiced eye had already alerted her that the baby needed swift medical attention.

The unrelenting hot weather wasn't helping the situation any. It wasn't the first time Leslie deplored both the lack of air conditioning in her battered car and the unexpected June heat wave, which had unfortunately coincided with her flight across the midwestern plains.

Oh well. Despite the fatigue that threatened to overwhelm her, she lifted her chin firmly. She would find Penny the help she needed right away, and then locate a nursing job for herself at a nearby hospital. She would make a life for the two of them here in Cincinnati. It was far enough from Chicago that Tony might never trace them.

It was almost dark by the time Leslie reached the downtown area, but luck was with her—there on the next block she saw a small flashing sign signaling a sidewalk clinic. With a sigh of relief she slid into a parking space, turned off the engine, and reached for Penny. The clinic seemed deserted, however; and as she approached it, she stared with dismay at the "Closed" sign hanging on the door. "Hmmm," she murmured to the fragile bundle on her shoulder. "Well, Penny love, *now* what do we do?"

As if in answer, the door suddenly flung open and a tall man, moving swiftly, nearly careened into Leslie. "Sorry," he apologized, slamming the door behind him and glancing at her. "The clinic's closed, miss."

Leslie looked up and met his impersonal stare, noting the white lab coat hanging open over neatly tailored slacks and a shirt, his identification tag hanging from his lapel. "Surely you can take just a minute to examine the baby, Doctor," she answered quickly before he could move around her. "We've been driving a long time, and—"

"Come back tomorrow and the doctor on duty will see to it." He dismissed her brusquely, but Leslie faced him squarely, blocking his path.

"This baby is ill, Doctor," she stated crisply, "and that ought to concern you—now. Or don't physicians take the Hippocratic oath anymore?"

The doctor's unusually light eyes flashed in surprise and then annoyance as he stared at her. Leslie lifted her chin, stood her ground, and was rewarded when he shrugged, turned back, and unlocked the clinic door.

"Put the child on that examining table," he told her over his shoulder as he headed for the sink to wash his hands again. "And be quick about it—I should have closed up an hour ago!"

"Yes, Doctor," Leslie replied smoothly, but her heart sank at his curt attitude. Why hadn't she been fortunate enough to meet an older, fatherly physician—someone patient and kind like several favorite surgeons with whom she'd trained—rather than this irritable man? If he was annoyed with her now, she could imagine his reaction once he saw what poor condition the baby was in! He would blame her, of course, even though she'd had nothing to do with Penny until this week. A wave of defensiveness swept across her, but she swallowed hard against it. She would say nothing to vex him further because Penny desperately needed his skill. And Penny was all that mattered right now.

As she undid the infant's thin sleeper, she studied the physician out of the corner of her eye. He was tall, lean, and looked to be about thirty, with wide shoulders that amply filled his surgical coat. Its whiteness emphasized the crisp ebony of his hair, a startling contrast to those light eyes. An arrogant nose, a firm chin bearing a deep cleft in the center completed the portrait of a man Leslie decided was ruggedly handsome in an unconventional sort of way. Handsome, yes, but as he turned and the cool blue eyes swept across her, she recoiled instinctively. A man like that—aloof, imperious—could also be extremely unpleasant to deal with.

He strode across the room to the table, and as he bent over Penny, Leslie noticed the name tag on his lapel: "Steven Sawyer, M.D." *Well, Dr. Sawyer,* she thought, taking a deep breath, *I imagine you'll be venting your rage on me at any moment.*

She didn't have long to wait. She had laid a cloth diaper across Penny's naked little body, but as Dr. Sawyer slipped it farther down, probing and turning the infant, she saw his jaw tense. "Unbelievable," he muttered. "This child has a rash that could have come only through neglect; she's pathetically undernourished." Efficiently, he swung Penny onto the scale. "Barely eight pounds. What was her birth weight?"

His abrupt question caught Leslie by surprise. "I . . . I'm not sure."

"You're not *sure*?" His dark head shot up, and he fastened the full force of his angry gaze upon her. "You *are* the child's mother, aren't you?"

Leslie had anticipated this question, but as it bounced across the empty room, the enormity of her masquerade stunned her. "I—yes, she's mine," she replied quietly, dropping her eyes. Well, it was true, wasn't it? she argued with herself. She had accepted responsibility for Penny back in that squalid Chicago tenement, and if this physician chose to assume she was her mother, so much the better.

She looked up again, conscious of a sudden silence, and realized that Dr. Sawyer was studying her closely. She could imagine the poor impression he was receiving from her loose, wind-blown hair, her rumpled clothes, the dark smudges of fatigue under her eyes. "And the baby's father?" he asked pointedly, looking at her ring finger, which bore no wedding band.

"I can't see that it's any business of yours," Leslie answered calmly, although her heart had started to pound.

"Obviously you can't see much of anything, it seems,"

Dr. Sawyer countered. "Not even how badly you've ne-glected your baby."

"That's a terrible accusation!" Leslie challenged him before she had a chance to think. "What right do you have to judge a person you don't even know?"

"I don't have to know *you*," he answered coldly. "I have this child as evidence of the kind of parent you must be. And you're lucky that her right hip is a birth defect rather than an injury, or I could have you investigated for child abuse!" His mouth tightened. "As a matter of fact—"

"Tell me about the hip," Leslie prodded urgently, swal-lowing the angry retort on her lips. She too had noticed Penny's oddly jutting leg, and no matter what Dr. Sawyer thought of her, she needed his expert advice.

"It's a flaw in the socket, and can probably be corrected with casts," he told her after a pause, his eyes still angry. "I'll give you the name of a good orthopedic man; that is, if you'd want to *bother* about it."

Leslie winced at his sarcasm, but held her tongue as he scrawled something on the back of a card, and also wrote several prescriptions and filled out a diet sheet. She knew she couldn't afford to arouse his wrath again, whatever he thought of her.

"Thank you, Dr. Sawyer," she murmured politely, reaching for the papers, but his fingers tightened on them, holding them just beyond her grasp. Startled, Leslie looked up at him.

"I'm going to give you just one warning," he said softly but firmly. "If I ever lay eyes on this child again in a similar condition, I won't hesitate to report you to the authorities. Is that clear?"

"Perfectly." Leslie tore the papers from his fingers, her temper finally exploding. "And you needn't worry, Doctor. I have absolutely no intention of asking for your help ever again. I can only hope you don't treat your regular patients with the same rudeness I've experienced!" With trembling fingers she reached for a fresh diaper for Penny, and for the first time the baby let out a frail whimper.

"Fortunately, I don't have to examine pathetic waifs like yours very often," Dr. Sawyer retorted, turning toward the sink. "I'm a general surgeon, not a pediatrician."

"Very impressive," Leslie murmured briskly, snapping Penny's sleeper. "I'm surprised you're wasting your valuable talents here at a street clinic, instead of making piles of money to go with your snobbish attitude!"

He turned suddenly, and Leslie saw to her surprise a glint of unexpected humor in his light eyes. "I thought you didn't approve of judging people without knowing them," he responded, and then as the hot blush stole to Leslie's cheeks, he actually grinned.

"But I . . . oh, never mind!" Leslie reached for her purse, hurled a bill on the table, and quickly gathered Penny into her arms. The next thing she knew, they were out on the darkened street. Dr. Sawyer closed the clinic door firmly and strode away from them.

As his footsteps faded, Leslie climbed into her car, opened the last disposable bottle of formula, and wearily nestled Penny in her arms. While Penny sucked contentedly, Leslie tried to calm down. The scene at the clinic had drained her small reserve of strength. She felt exhausted beyond belief, overwhelmed at the responsibility just laid on her slender shoulders, and not at all sure that she would have the stamina to cope with what lay ahead.

It was amazing what the human body could endure, she reflected. Just last week she had been a patient in the same Minnesota hospital where she worked, recovering from an especially virulent strain of flu. It was then that she received Lee's letter—delayed because of Leslie's hospitalization—and its compelling message had pushed her out of the sick-

bed and onto the highway. On to Chicago, and to her troubled twin sister.

Lee ... through Leslie's grief came the image of her
only sibling—teasing, always in trouble, the bane of the
kindly grandmother who'd raised them both after their parents' deaths so many years ago. Almost identical in looks,
the twins had been opposite in personality, with serious, du-
tiful Leslie somehow eclipsed in the background while vi-
vacious Lee took center stage. They had shared a certain
sisterly fondness, but had never been true soul mates. Leslie
had gone off to nursing college with a sense of guilty relief,
glad that Lee had other goals—an eventual modeling job in
Chicago and a separate life.

And yet Leslie had missed her twin, the force of Lee's
personality, her bubbly enthusiasm that would surely cap-
tivate the entire Second City.

Yet things hadn't gone Lee's way. At first her infrequent
letters had been excited, but soon the tone had turned to
disillusionment. Modeling jobs were hard to find, she wrote,
unless one knew the right people. Leslie, immersed in her
studies, had grown increasingly uneasy about Lee's appar-
ent choice of companions. She seemed to know all the *wrong*
people—drug users, producers of cheap films, proprietors
of establishments on the edges of society. Then there was
Tony. Lee had sent a blurred snapshot of the two of them
once, and Leslie had shuddered involuntarily at the image
of the large, rough-looking man who was now a presumed
part of her twin's life.

After receiving the photo, Leslie wrote, suggesting that
she come and visit (and hopefully, investigate Lee's lifestyle), but it had been the wrong approach, for Lee's letters
stopped. Although she sent flowers when their grandmother
died, Lee didn't return to Minnesota for the funeral. It was
left to Leslie, by now working in surgery and maintaining
her own small apartment, to dispose of Gram's belongings

and say the final farewells. On an impulse, she had sent Lee Gram's worn and treasured Bible, hoping against hope that her sister would read it and discover there were better, richer ways to live her life. The Bible had never been returned, but Leslie's subsequent letters came back, marked "Addressee Unknown."

Then unexpectedly last week, out of the blue, she received Lee's terse, almost frantic note: "Leslie—I've had the baby, and I'm sick, really sick. Please take her and don't let Tony find her. I know I can count on you. I always could."

Had it been only a few days ago? Holding Penny on her shoulder for a final burp, Leslie closed her eyes now and thought again of the decrepit, run-down brownstone where she'd found the baby and forever lost her sister. She'd climbed the filthy staircase, cringing as she stepped on roaches, and knocked at the second-floor apartment. "Lee?" she'd called hesitantly, appalled at the dismal surroundings. "Lee, it's me, Leslie."

Slowly the door had swung open, and Leslie faced a disheveled teenage girl, whose eyes squinted as she surveyed Leslie. "She said you'd come," the girl said finally. "You look just like Lee did."

"Lee . . . did?" Leslie repeated in bewilderment. "You mean, she isn't here anymore?"

The girl ran a bare toe across a floorboard, long hair hiding her expression. "Lee's dead," she said bluntly.

"Dead!" Leslie heard herself cry as she gripped the doorway. "But . . . but when? How?"

A baby's wail pierced the silence, and the girl's expression—blank until now—softened slightly in an attitude of sympathy. "Died after Penny was born last month," she murmured. "She made us promise not to call a doctor, kept saying she'd be better soon, and then—" The baby's cry rose and the girl turned. "You'd better come in," she said over her shoulder.

Numb and bewildered, Leslie stepped into a dim, dirty room ringed with broken furniture and thick with stale food and a peculiar odor—the unmistakable aroma of pot. This was where her sister had died—and presumably lived? The thought was unbearable. "But how. . . ?" she started, then stopped as the girl approached and laid a damp blanket-wrapped bundle in her arms.

"This is Penny," she said. "You'd better take her before Tony finds out."

"Wait a minute! Who are you?" Leslie heard her own voice rise again, and knew that shock and grief were taking hold. She couldn't afford to lose control now, not when she needed some answers. She took a deep breath. "Tell me about my sister and Tony—you," she said firmly. "Were they married?"

The girl shrugged. "Name's Sandy. A bunch of us been living here together. And Tony . . ." She lit a cigarette. "Tony was Lee's man. He went to jail on a drug bust or something . . . I don't know. But when he gets out . . ." She shrugged her shoulders.

"When he gets out—what?" Leslie prodded.

There was silence while Sandy stared into space, considering Leslie's question. "Tony's bad," she responded at last. "After he went to jail, Lee was scared and decided to go home to you for a while."

"And then. . . ?" Leslie resisted the impulse to shake the girl out of her lethargy. "Why didn't she leave?"

"She was sick almost all the time. We tried to take care of her. . . ." The thin voice trailed off. It was like talking to a wisp of fog, but Leslie had to find some answers about her sister.

"Maybe it would be better if we turned Penny over to the authorities, Sandy."

For the first time during the bizarre conversation, Sandy reacted. "They'd put her in one foster home after another," she said quickly. "That's how I was raised." As she came closer, Leslie could see a glint of tears in her eyes. "Look at me!" she demanded. "Do you want Penny to grow up like me?"

Leslie felt an unexpected twinge of sympathy for the girl. Though she was young, troubled, and vulnerable, she and her friends had cared for Penny, however ineptly, after Lee's death.

"You've got to take her!" Sandy had suddenly whirled and dragged a shopping bag out from behind the couch. "Her clothes are here"—she rummaged through the pitifully small store of contents—"and we've been keeping her in that portable bed over there. And look—Lee said this was for you." Her thin hand held the old Bible Leslie had sent.

"She *did* get it." Leslie felt a poignant pang of gratitude. "I wonder if she ever read it."

"She did. She was holding it when . . . when she died." The girl blinked back tears, crammed the Bible in the bag, and shoved it toward Leslie. "Take it—take everything and get out!" she said with sudden urgency. "Tony could show up at any time!"

Leslie looked around the apartment in a torment of confusion. Wasn't it illegal to steal an infant from its father? Would the authorities come after her if they knew? But what kind of life lay before her newfound niece if she were raised in this sordid and probably dangerous environment? And would a series of foster homes be any better?

Steady, reliable, law-abiding Leslie had suddenly tightened her grasp on the baby—and fled.

———

She stretched her legs now, cramped in the car's interior, and Penny, sleeping on her shoulder, gave a contented sigh. Leslie's arms tightened around the tiny bundle, and from somewhere deep within her—through layers of grief, bewilderment, and fatigue—came a small glow of hope.

Well, what else could I do, Lord? she said. *Penny's your daughter, too, isn't she? And whatever I do to the least of your children . . .*

She had made her decision and burned all her bridges—phoning in her resignation from the Minnesota hospital staff and canceling her apartment lease, for Tony would surely know where she lived and worked. Penny was hers now. She would find a job and a place to stay and begin to build a new life for both of them. She could do it, and somehow, with God's guidance, she would.

Glancing toward the clinic, darkened now on the deserted street, her thoughts returned to the rude Dr. Steven Sawyer. "Well, there's one bright spot in our topsy-turvy world, Penny," she murmured to the downy, copper-colored head on her shoulder. "At least we'll never see *him* again."

She laid Penny gently in her car seat and started the car.

2

$\mathcal{L}$eslie filled the last of the medication cups, glancing hastily at the clock. Two in the afternoon—right on schedule, and only an hour to go until her shift ended. Picking up the tray, she started toward the still-unfamiliar ward hallway, but Mrs. Ames, the head nurse, stopped her.

"I'll do those, Leslie," she said kindly. "Why don't you sit down for a moment and handle the phones. You're looking a bit peaked."

Gratefully, Leslie surrendered the trays. "It's this heat wave," she smiled ruefully. "I guess I haven't adjusted to it yet."

"It *is* unusually warm for June," the older woman soothed, although Leslie noticed a slight frown on her face. "Don't worry, you'll get used to it."

But would she? Leslie sighed as she slumped into a chair by the phone. Would she ever get used to caring for a baby—an uncomfortable baby now in casts, who whimpered most of the night and needed to be held and comforted? And then, with only a few hours of rest, working a long and demanding shift in an unfamiliar hospital? Would she ever adjust to the depressing furnished flat she had quickly rented in one of Cincinnati's questionable neighborhoods? Although Leslie had scrubbed and polished every inch of it, hung posters and plants to brighten it, the rooms were light-years away from what she would have chosen, had there been a choice.

Would she ever get used to the sad, haunting dreams that seemed to plague her, the loss of a sister who, despite their differences, had been a part of herself? She battled fear over Tony and what he or the authorities might do to her if they found Penny in her care.

And yet things had been going well, she reflected, very well, as if the Lord had kept a protective hand on her shoulder throughout the whole ordeal. It had been only a week since she'd arrived in Cincinnati, but Penny had already had her corrective casts put on in an outpatient ward connected with St. Luke's Hospital. And when the orthopedist had discovered Leslie was a nurse, he sent her immediately to the personnel department. "Good experienced nurses are in short supply, Mrs. Bennett," he had assured her. "Especially those trained in surgery like you."

Mrs. Bennett. Leslie shook her head sadly as she hung up the ward phone. The physician had simply assumed she was married and Penny was her daughter. She had gone along with his assumption despite her feelings of guilt. Her tender conscience resisted the idea of a lie, no matter how necessary it seemed. But as long as Penny belonged to her, she felt compelled to play the part.

However, Leslie had decided it was important that she keep Penny's existence a secret from her co-workers. Nurses might be in demand, but she was sure the personnel department wouldn't approve of her exhausting schedule and the detrimental effect it might have on her efficiency at work. No, she'd have to tread warily and hide Penny as carefully from the nurses as from the elusive and menacing Tony. It wouldn't do to lose her job; the baby was depending on her.

Suddenly Leslie remembered the frown she'd noticed on Mrs. Ames' face just now. Had it been directed at her? Had she made any mistakes this week, anything serious enough to jeopardize her job? Quickly she reviewed the day, and just then the head nurse dropped heavily into the chair opposite her.

"Whew—what an afternoon!" Mrs. Ames sighed wearily. "Seven new admissions, and Mr. Parker in thirty-one B having a nervous collapse over his heart surgery tomorrow."

"He's a sweet old man; I'll look in on him before I go off duty," Leslie offered. "Sometimes it calms a surgical patient just to talk about his fears, don't you think?"

"I do." Mrs. Ames looked at her keenly. "You're a good nurse, Leslie, and I'm glad you wound up on this floor, even though you'd probably rather be working in surgery."

"Why . . . thank you." Leslie smiled at the unexpected praise. "It's true I have experience in the operating room, but I'm on the waiting list for the next opening. And until then, well, you've been very good to me, Mrs. Ames, and I appreciate it."

"There's just one thing I'd like to discuss," Mrs. Ames began, and the frown, Leslie noticed uneasily, was back on her face. "I've been wondering—"

"Mrs. Ames," a firm but friendly voice interrupted, "I can't seem to find the Prentice chart."

Leslie froze, her back to the voice. Where had she heard it before?

"I had it out just now." Mrs. Ames rose swiftly with no sign of her previous fatigue. "There it is, Dr. Sawyer."

Dr. Sawyer! That terrible physician at the clinic! Did *he* work at St. Luke's? The phone jangled and Leslie gratefully grabbed the receiver, keeping her head averted. Surely he wouldn't recognize or remember her. She looked different, she reminded herself frantically, in a crisp white uniform, with long red-gold hair wound in an efficient coil. She listened with half an ear to the speaker on the other end while the rest of her strained to control a sudden panic. What if Dr. Sawyer recognized her and demanded to know what she was doing here, or loudly accused her again of mistreating the baby? If he chose to expose her, she realized she wouldn't be able to get a nursing job anywhere in the city.

Leslie bent her head over the desk, busily noting the telephone message on a pad, and was conscious of a silence behind her. Dr. Sawyer must have gone while she was on the phone. Relieved, and feeling her pounding heart slow, she swung around in time to see the dark-haired man walking away from the nurses' station. "That was close," Leslie murmured under her breath, when suddenly Dr. Sawyer stopped, wheeled around, and came striding back. She ducked her head quickly, but not before his eyes swept past her and then returned. Busily Leslie retied her shoe while a nervous flush darkened her pale cheeks. Surely he wouldn't remember . . .

"Anything else, Dr. Sawyer?" Leslie heard Mrs. Ames ask from the chart section.

"Nope, just forgot my pen," he answered casually, then stood looking for a moment—Leslie was sure of it—directly at her. She retied her other shoe, keeping her face averted; and finally, to her relief, she heard him turn again and stride briskly down the hall.

"Well!" Mrs. Ames smiled from across the station. "Dr. Sawyer certainly took his time staring at you."

"Really?" Leslie laughed lightly. "I didn't notice him."

"He's hard to miss," Mrs. Ames pointed out dreamily. "That cleft in his chin, and those light blue eyes . . ."

"Why, Mrs. Ames," Leslie laughed again, this time in genuine amusement, "and you, a married woman!"

"Marriage hasn't dulled my eyesight," Mrs. Ames told her with mock severity, "and it has nothing to do with admiring a truly good-looking man. Although his entire fan club here is wasting its time."

"Really?"

Mrs. Ames nodded. "He's spoken for, we hear. Some society lady named Rita Marchand got her long fingernails into him a while back. They broke up once, I understand, but rumor has it that a wedding is a distinct possibility."

"Well, that's nice." Leslie shrugged with what she hoped was disinterest. Actually, despite her mistrust of Steven Sawyer, she found herself inexplicably wanting to know more about him.

"Well, maybe yes and maybe no," the head nurse mused. "He can't be marrying her for her money—his own practice has real potential, even though it's new. And he wouldn't do anything as insincere as that anyway. It must be love, and yet . . ."

"And yet?" Leslie prodded in spite of herself.

"Well, I've met Rita Marchand at a few staff parties because her father is on the hospital's board of directors, and she's a real snob. I can't see her attracting anyone as kind and decent as Steven Sawyer."

Kind and decent? Leslie bit her tongue in astonished fury. Were they talking about the same man?

"Oh, he has a quick temper," Mrs. Ames went on as if she had read Leslie's mind, "but there's a heart of gold underneath that rough exterior."

"Of course." Leslie reached under the desk for her purse before saying something she shouldn't. "My shift's over, Mrs. Ames, so I'll stop in to see Mr. Parker on the way out, all right?"

"As soon as I tell you what I've been meaning to say all day." Mrs. Ames came toward her with the worried frown back in place, and Leslie's heart sank. But Mrs. Ames didn't look angry, just concerned.

"Leslie, dear," she began, "while your work is everything it should be and even more, I can't help feeling that you're under some sort of strain. It shows in your face, you know—those dark circles under your eyes and a thinness about you that doesn't seem natural. I'm not trying to pry, but nursing is a demanding job. Are you sure you're up to it—both emotionally and physically?"

Relief swept through Leslie, accompanied by an over-whelming need to tell her motherly superior the whole truth. It would be such a relief to unburden herself, to be completely honest and share the lonely load she had been carrying. But common sense intervened, and she realized there was too much to lose. If Mrs. Ames discovered that she had so recently been a patient herself, she might insist that she rest longer before resuming her work. And if any-one found out about her sleepless nights with a cranky new-born, and her upsetting dreams . . .

Leslie had always been able to draw upon an inner faith, and she knew that despite her exhausting schedule, she would never shortchange the patients in her care. But the hospital staff didn't know her, and she couldn't risk that their opinion might conflict with hers.

"I'm fine, Mrs. Ames, really I am," she assured her worried superior. "Moving here took more out of me than I expected." *That* was surely an understatement! "But I promise I'll look more like myself before long." She flashed a dimple, and was relieved to see an answering smile from Mrs. Ames.

"I doubt that you could improve on *those* looks!" the older nurse grinned. "What I wouldn't give for that creamy skin, those big brown eyes—oh, get on with you!"

Leslie laughed as she went down the hall. She was al-ways genuinely surprised when people admired her looks. She had never thought of herself as pretty—when she thought about the subject at all—but there was no account-ing for people's tastes.

She reached Mr. Parker's room and peeked inside, dis-tressed to see that the elderly man was nervously twisting the edge of the bed sheet. "Mr. Parker?" she called quietly from the door. "I'm going off duty now, but I came to say I'll be praying for you tomorrow during your operation."

The old man's face brightened. His eyes, though blue and sharp, were set deep in folds of wrinkled skin, tanned and lined like the shell of a walnut, and they met hers in an attitude of hope. "Really?" he asked, and Leslie noticed that a worn Bible lay on the table near his bed. "Are you a Christian?"

"I sure am." She came and sat on the side of his bed, her hand closing over his. "My grandmother saw to that, and I'll always be grateful to her." Mr. Parker left his fragile fingers in her warm grasp, and the two of them looked comfortably at each other. "It won't be so bad," she told him quietly. "You've been awfully sick, but bypass surgery is going to make a new man out of you, honestly."

"So they say," he mused. "And I have a lot of living yet to do, Miss Bennett. But a man can't help but be afraid . . . sometimes."

"I know." She tightened her fingers around his, then looked again at the old Bible, so much like Gram's. "Would . . . would you like to say the twenty-third Psalm with me?" she asked hesitantly. "I always say it whenever I'm afraid, and perhaps—"

"It's my favorite," Mr. Parker told her, and for the first time a trace of a smile flitted across his features.

"The Lord is my shepherd," Leslie began softly. "I shall not want. He maketh me to lie down in green pastures. . . ."

"He leadeth me beside the still waters," Mr. Parker answered, his voice firmer. Together they recited the comforting words of Scripture, and at their conclusion, an expression of peace had replaced the old man's worried frown. Leslie bent impulsively and kissed the wrinkled cheek, and as she did so, Mr. Parker looked past her. "Why, hello, Dr. Steve," he said, genuinely pleased to see him.

Not again! Leslie froze. It had to be Dr. Sawyer. And how long had he been listening to them?

"Hello, Jed," came the familiar voice from the doorway, now edged with affection. "I just stopped in to see if you had any questions about tomorrow, or if I could set your mind at rest."

"No need," Mr. Parker sighed contentedly, "thanks to this little girl here. She's a real treasure, Doc."

"Yes," Dr. Sawyer replied smoothly. "She's certainly one of our favorites."

He was baiting her, Leslie thought angrily as she fumbled for her purse, gave the old man's hand another squeeze, and rose swiftly. If she could just slide past Dr. Sawyer and get out of the hospital before anything else happened.

Keeping her eyes averted, she managed to move around his tall frame and was out in the hall and halfway down the stairs—free at last!—before a firm hand gripped her shoulder and swung her around against the stair bannister. Shocked, she looked up into the penetrating blue eyes of her tormentor.

"So it *is* you!" Dr. Sawyer's expression was incredulous. "I thought you looked familiar at the nurses' station, but I wouldn't have believed—"

"Believed what?" she challenged him, upset at his intrusion. "I'm a qualified nurse, with every right to be here!"

"I can't accept that," he shot back, and Leslie could see that his anger was rising to meet hers. "No nurse would treat a baby the way you did."

Her heart sank. Would his unjust accusations never cease? And would he now expose her, cause her to lose her job? Tears of fear and exhaustion sprang to her eyes and trembled on her long lashes. "Please . . ." she whispered, "please just leave me alone!" Quickly she wheeled and ran down the rest of the steps. She didn't look back, but knew that he watched her all the way to the parking lot.

Leslie's heart didn't stop hammering until she was almost in front of her apartment. Her secret was exposed now, and she had no doubt that the judgmental Dr. Sawyer would waste no time reporting her to both Mrs. Ames and the personnel department. By tomorrow she'd probably be out of a job again, and how would she pay the rest of Penny's medical bills, to say nothing of food and rent and. . . ?

She sighed as she maneuvered her battered little car into a parking space on the cluttered and grimy avenue. She had faced difficult times before, and she could do it again. But it would help, she admitted sadly, if she felt physically stronger. That pervasive weakness that lingered from her hospitalization, a fatigue that quickly seemed to sap whatever energy she could muster, added to the tension and grief she'd recently experienced. Mrs. Ames had been right. Leslie wasn't up to the rigors of nursing, at least not yet.

But she had to be; that's all there was to it. Reluctantly, she climbed the boardinghouse steps, entered the dismal hallway, and checked the battered table for mail. Still no letter from Sandy, the little teenager at Lee's old apartment. Leslie had written to her the day she found her nursing job, enclosing some money and a request that Sandy see if Penny had a birth certificate on file, and if so, to mail a copy to her. It had been a risk to let anyone know where she was, but she had faith in Sandy's innate decency, if not her current state of mind, and the certificate was important. Perhaps Sandy was strung out on drugs and couldn't handle the request. If so, Leslie hoped fervently that the teenager had destroyed her letter before anyone else read it.

She knocked on the first-floor door, which was quickly opened by Mrs. Briggs, the boardinghouse landlady. With her too-short nose, protruding eyes, and perpetually irritated expression, Mrs. Briggs always reminded Leslie of a scowling Pekinese, and today the frown was even more obvious.

"That baby's been fussing all day," Mrs. Briggs announced grimly. "Couldn't hear my TV shows. Don't know how much longer I can care for her, Mrs. Bennett."

"I know it's a tough job, Mrs. Briggs." Leslie offered a sympathy that was less than genuine. If Mrs. Briggs would only hold Penny occasionally and give her some attention rather than, as Leslie suspected, leaving her to cry all day in her portable bed, she would be fine. "It's only until her casts come off, you know, and then I can take her to the day-care center." She handed Mrs. Briggs a folded bill, payment for another day's care that was probably no better than what Penny had endured in Chicago, and was rewarded by a reluctant and toothy grin.

"Oh, I guess a few more weeks can't hurt none," Mrs. Briggs condescended, pushing back a wisp of lank hair. "She's kind of cute at that. Puny, though." She left the doorway and Leslie stepped in behind her, wrinkling her nose at the dank smell of tobacco and cooking grease. Mrs. Briggs returned, depositing Penny in Leslie's arms, then proceeded to carry the bed and diaper bag up two flights of stairs to Leslie's third-floor rooms.

Leslie followed her slowly. Each step seemed an effort, and the higher she went, the more oppressive the heat and stale hallway odors became. Penny was soaking wet, still wearing the thin garment Leslie had dressed her in that morning. Didn't the landlady ever think to change a baby's wet clothes? A sense of helplessness overcame her, but she thrust it back. Mrs. Briggs was better than no sitter at all; and until Leslie was more securely settled, she couldn't risk losing her.

"Thank you, Mrs. Briggs," she said, trying to be courteous as she reached the top of the stairs. "I'll see you tomorrow."

"Why, sure," the landlady responded, friendly now that she was relinquishing her small charge. "Penny and me get along just fine, don't we, sweetheart?"

Penny began to cry, and Leslie pushed open her door with the last ounce of strength she possessed. The heat that had been building all day in the airless rooms reached her like the blast of a furnace, and it was all she could do to close the door behind her, reach the dingy couch just a few feet away, lay Penny down, and stretch out beside her.

Penny whimpered, and Leslie reached out to stroke her soft cheek. "In a minute, Penny," she murmured. "Wait a bit, my love, until your mommy gets her second wind."

Mommy. The enormity of her responsibility settled upon her once again like a heavy cloak. She thought of Dr. Sawyer and his bitter, disparaging accusations, the pleasure he was probably now experiencing as he tore her career to shreds. She thought of slovenly Mrs. Briggs, into whose dubious care she must entrust Penny, and the dismal apartment, the depressing neighborhood without so much as a leafy tree to break the monotony. And her checkbook balance, hovering precariously near zero, and her aching limbs and relentless fatigue that drained her body and her spirit.

It was too much for anyone to bear. The tears that had unexpectedly surfaced during her encounter with Steven Sawyer rose again, but she pushed them back. She would not give in. Somehow, in a way still unknown to her, she would find the strength she needed to go on.

"The Lord is my shepherd," she whispered to the lonely room. "I shall not want. . . ."

3

 *T*wo days passed, days during which Leslie walked a tightrope of anxiety and tension, waiting to be summoned to the personnel office, waiting for the look of deep disappointment on Mrs. Ames' face as she said, "I'm so sorry, my dear, but . . ." Yet nothing happened. It was inconceivable to her that Dr. Sawyer had not lodged a formal complaint against her, but he had apparently not done so, nor did he put in an appearance on her floor. By the weekend, with two full days to enjoy away from the hospital, Leslie was beginning to breathe a bit more easily. For whatever reason, Dr. Sawyer had decided to grant her a reprieve. And if she took pains never to cross his path again, he might forget she even existed. Surely, between his rising professional status, his wealthy fiancée and the high society life they probably enjoyed, Dr. Sawyer had other things to think about!

Leslie bought a secondhand collapsible stroller and spent Saturday afternoon on a blanket at the park with Penny. That evening she was pleased to see a slight pink bloom on the baby's cheeks. Penny was definitely looking better. Her rash was almost gone (although it was a continuing battle to make Mrs. Briggs use the salve), and with proper nutrition and vitamins, her frail body had finally started to fill out.

Sunday night, as Leslie was talking softly and tucking her into the car seat, Penny waved a tiny fist—and smiled!

"Oh, honey . . ." Leslie's eyes filled with sudden tears of happiness. For the first time she actually felt like a mother. Her continual fatigue and worry over finances were a small price to pay for such a reward.

Leslie's spirits were so high she almost bounced into the hospital on Monday morning, to be met by Mrs. Ames quickly reshuffling the schedule. "Oh, Leslie, I'm glad you're early." The head nurse waved her over to the station. "I've just had a call from surgery. There's an emergency gall bladder coming up now, and they're short a nurse—someone had to leave. Since you've had experience in O.R., would you mind filling in?"

"Not a bit," Leslie reassured her. "It will give me a chance to look in on Mr. Parker, too. I haven't seen him since Friday."

"He's recovering very well," Mrs. Ames replied, "but I wish I could say the same about *you.* Frankly, you look thinner and more tired now than you did when you took this job. Are you sure you're all right?"

"I'm fine," Leslie smiled, although she knew her superior was right. *I need a stretch in Intensive Care,* she thought ruefully as she headed for the elevator.

The surgical floor was just as Leslie remembered it from her days in Minnesota. She noticed two patients lightly sedated on gurneys in the hall, apparently waiting for operating rooms one and two, and a third man, probably the emergency gall bladder, being prepared for room three. Leslie showed her pass to the O.R. superintendent and was sent immediately to the scrub area. "Boy, am I glad to see you!" a dark-haired woman in greens sighed with relief. "I haven't had time to check the equipment yet, or—"

"Why don't you go ahead and do that?" Leslie suggested, moving quickly to the sink. "I'll be ready in ten minutes, and then I'll come in and help you."

"Great," her partner replied. "You know how Dr. Sawyer hates to be kept waiting."

Dr. Sawyer. Oh no! Leslie's pale face, reflected in the mirror above the sink, grew even whiter. Of all the terrible coincidences, to have to work with the very man she was trying so hard to avoid! *Why* hadn't she remembered he was a general surgeon? She could easily have refused the O.R. assignment.

But it was too late now. A good nurse never let her personal problems interfere with a critically ill patient's needs. Sighing, Leslie finished her scrub and checked to see that all her red-gold hair was hidden under the sterile cap. With its distinctive color concealed, and the surgical mask covering her features, perhaps Dr. Sawyer wouldn't even notice her.

Adjusting her gloves, she went quickly into the operating room where the anesthesiologist was bending over his patient, talking in a soothing tone. Dr. Sawyer, she noticed, was conversing with his resident while glancing at the instrument tray. "Are we ready?" he asked the room at large. "Where's my scrub nurse?"

"There she is." Leslie's partner pointed at her, and scurried around to the other side of the table near the cardiac monitor.

"Me?" Leslie asked, dismayed. The last thing she wanted to do was to stand across from Steven Sawyer and pass him the instruments he needed. Far safer was the circulating nurse position, moving around the operating room out of his line of vision.

"Are you new here?" Dr. Sawyer asked Leslie pleasantly, obviously trying to place her. "I don't think you and I have—"

"I'm a sub from another floor, Doctor," Leslie replied crisply, deciding to behave as confidently as possible. After all, there was no reason to assume he'd recognize her. "I have a background in O.R."

"Very well. Let's get started." He turned to check the patient's vital signs with the anesthesiologist while Leslie positioned herself across from him and looked at the instrument tray. Had she been away from O.R. too long? Would she remember everything that had to be done?

But she needn't have worried. When the surgery started, a part of her mind that had been lying dormant for the past several weeks suddenly snapped to attention. She knew exactly what to do, and her nimble fingers never faltered; if anything, she could anticipate Dr. Sawyer's commands before he uttered them.

"Knife."

"Knife, Doctor."

"Sponge."

"Sponge."

He was excellent, she noticed with a respect she had reserved for only a few surgeons. The operation was routine, but Dr. Sawyer had a quick deft touch and a skillful technique. She caught her breath once in a murmur of admiration, and knew that he had heard her. A moment later when she again anticipated his command and pressed the proper item into his hand, his eyes, tense with concentration, relaxed for a moment and flicked briefly to hers. "Thank you, Nurse."

"You're welcome," she answered smoothly, but her cheeks burned. An obviously talented surgeon who was also nice to his assistant—one didn't come across that combination too often. It was truly a shame that she knew his courtesy to be nothing more than a facade. The arrogant manner, the censorious attitude—that was the *real* Steven Sawyer, and she would do well to remember it.

Surgery ended, the patient was wheeled to recovery, and Dr. Sawyer followed, chart in hand. Leslie offered a prayer of gratitude. He hadn't noticed her, after all.

"Sorry to stick you with scrub nurse duty," her partner commented as she and Leslie cleared the room, "but Dr. Sawyer makes me nervous. He's such a perfectionist."

"I would hope so," Leslie responded dryly as she stripped the operating table. "In surgery, it certainly helps."

The other nurse laughed. "I'm not talking about his ability. It's just that he routinely expects the best, not only from himself but from everyone around him. His standards are almost too high."

Leslie thought of his bruising comments at the clinic and winced. She was glad she had done a decent job today. If Steven Sawyer found fault with her professional behavior, well . . . it didn't bear thinking about.

"What do we do next?" she asked her partner. "Is there another operation scheduled?"

"Not for half an hour." The girl looked at the clock. "You've got time for a cup of coffee if you like."

"Is Dr. Sawyer—?"

"Relax," her partner grinned. "He's in room two next. You'll be here with me for the rest of the day."

"Good." Leslie took off her top set of greens and headed down the hall. She'd forego the coffee, she decided, in favor of a quick visit with Mr. Parker, if he was still on the surgical wing.

She discovered as she checked the charts he still was, and went toward his room. Rounding the corner, however, she stopped dead in her tracks. Coming from Mr. Parker's room was the unmistakable sound of Steven Sawyer's voice.

"I know it sounds unbelievable, Jed," Steven was saying in an exasperated tone, "but there it is. Another helper has left, and she's all alone again."

"So that's where you've been for the last four days, trying to pick up the pieces." A weak chuckle from Mr. Parker.

"That makes three women since the beginning of the year, don't it?"

"Four. I can't blame them. Aunt Mae is a terrible patient, and it's a lonely, desolate place. . . ."

There was a silence. Ashamed, yet curious, Leslie inched forward. "It's a beautiful place, and you know it, boy," said Mr. Parker again, talking sternly as if he were lecturing a child. "Wild and quiet, with them hills reaching up to the heavens. Tarnation, boy, you know why Miss Mae is being so difficult. She wants *you*, back where you belong."

Another silence followed, then Steven cleared his throat. "You know that's impossible, Jed. My work is here, in Cincinnati."

"Your work is anywhere a good doctor like you wants it to be," Mr. Parker reproved him gently. "No, boy, if you was honest, you'd admit that that little filly's got you by the nose and—"

"That's enough, Jed!" Leslie heard the warning tone in Steven's voice, turned and walked away from the doorway as fast as she could. She had no desire to be anywhere nearby if the famous Sawyer temper was about to explode, and from all indications, it wouldn't be long. But Dr. Sawyer wouldn't abuse a sick elderly man like Mr. Parker, would he? And yet the two of them seemed on familiar and comfortable terms, born of long years together. It was certainly a puzzle, as the rest of their conversation had been. She had no right to eavesdrop either. Whatever had possessed her? And—Leslie stopped short, and felt a tremor shoot through her. Mr. Parker said that Steven had been gone for four days! *That* was why he hadn't reported Leslie to the hospital authorities—he had been out of town with someone called Aunt Mae. But now that he was back, it could only be a matter of time. . . . Oh, why had she eavesdropped and burst her little bubble of security?

There was no time to mull over this latest dilemma, for

the next surgical patient was already waiting outside O.R. three. Leslie stepped briskly around the gurney, scrubbed and dressed again, and helped her partner prepare the room. Now was no time to let her mind wander, not with another operation due to begin at any moment. She'd worry about it all later.

Once again her instincts took over, and she chose the instruments with precision, following the unfamiliar surgeon's brusque commands with efficiency. "Good work," he told her gruffly as the patient was being wheeled to recovery.

"You are good," the other nurse commented as they cleared the room again. "Where did you train?"

"In Minnesota. How about you?" Leslie's question was born out of politeness rather than interest, for now that the tension of surgery had again passed, she felt the aftereffects—a slight headache, pain between her shoulder blades, her body limp as a rag doll's. Regretfully she recalled previous days in Minnesota when she could assist at one operation after another, keeping fatigue at bay until evening. Now, however, perhaps due to her lingering weariness, she was ready to call it quits after just a few hours. *Pull yourself together,* she warned herself sternly, *or Steven Sawyer won't have to see that you're fired—you'll lose the job all by yourself.*

Leslie's companion had been chatting brightly about her own background when suddenly she stiffened. "Oh, oh," she murmured to Leslie, "look who's coming back."

The broad-shouldered figure of Steven Sawyer loomed past the glass doors; he was obviously conferring with the O.R. supervisor.

"He's not going to operate with us again, is he?" Leslie was seized with alarm. She could remain anonymous once, perhaps, but twice? Just then the supervisor stuck her head in the door. "We've got a change here, ladies," she barked.

"You, the substitute, assist Dr. Sawyer in room two now. Your replacement is on her way."

"Wow, he really must like your style," Leslie's partner whispered, intrigued. "I've never known Dr. Sawyer to *request* a nurse."

"And I wish he hadn't today! Is my hair hidden?" Leslie asked the nurse in panic. If he even caught a glimpse of it . . .

"Relax," the girl giggled. "Dr. Sawyer isn't *that* picky."

If it were only that simple . . . Leslie went down the hall to room two, her knees shaking. As always, she whispered a prayer for the patient, the surgeon's skill, and her own competence, then finished with a plea, "And don't let him recognize me, Lord, please!"

She needn't have worried. Everything was in readiness, and Dr. Sawyer was leaning over a young groggy boy with—Leslie glanced at the chart—an acute case of appendicitis. "And we promise not to let anything happen to you," Dr. Sawyer reassured the child gently. "See, here's a nice nurse who's going to help me make your tummy all better."

Drawn by the child's fear, Leslie moved close to the table. "I'll bet you're feeling pretty scared right now, aren't you, honey?" she murmured kindly.

The boy's tearful eyes met hers. "Everyone tells me to be brave," he said plaintively, yawning in spite of himself, "but . . ."

"But it's hard, isn't it?" Leslie nodded. "Tell you what—why don't you take a little nap while we're getting ready here? We'll wake you if we need you."

The boy sighed. "Well, okay . . ." Calmer now, his eyes were already closing as the anesthesiologist administered the injection, and within a few minutes everything was ready.

Leslie pressed the first instrument into Dr. Sawyer's hand as he made a perfect incision. Once again, she forgot her exhaustion in the familiar challenge of keeping illness at bay. Calmly and quickly she kept pace with the surgeon's moves, almost ahead of him as he signaled for clamp or stat. "Fine," he murmured once, "we got here just in time."

Leslie didn't respond—the less said, the better. Besides, her headache had worked into a throbbing giant of pain, taking all her ebbing strength to keep going. Once, her hand trembled slightly, but she controlled it immediately, and was sure no one had noticed. Dr. Sawyer was stapling now, and soon she could leave . . . get an aspirin . . . and go home to take care of Penny. . . .

It was over. The circulating nurse wheeled the little patient out of the room to recovery, followed by the resident and anesthesiologist. Leslie paused, waiting for Dr. Sawyer to follow suit so she could take off her mask and sit down for a moment before stripping the room. Instead, he stood in front of her, peeling off his gloves. "You have a nice touch for patients as well as surgeons, Nurse," he said in a friendly tone. "I have surgery two days each week—is there any chance you could become my regular assistant?"

"I . . ." Leslie had started to perspire, half in dread and half because something odd was suddenly happening to her body. An aching blackness seemed to be impinging on the outer reaches of her eyes, creating a kind of tunnel vision where Dr. Sawyer was distant and unreal. She could hear him questioning her, but the words weren't penetrating through the pain. "I . . . I don't think so . . ." she began.

"Here, you're not going to faint, are you?" Dr. Sawyer stared at her in alarm, then strode forward and pulled off her mask and cap, dislodging the pins in her hair. As the red-gold curtain cascaded across his hand, he met her eyes in astonishment. "You!"

Leslie's head was light and as hollow as an empty eggshell. Then the blackness became complete, and her last conscious thought was Steven Sawyer's look of startled comprehension as she pitched forward into his arms.

"Nurse Bennett . . . Bennett, wake up!" Someone was patting her cheek and she coughed, blinked and focused on that familiar light blue gaze. "Better?" he asked, his eyes showing concern.

He had been kneeling on the floor, holding her, she realized now, for his arms were firm around her, and her cheek lay against the rough fabric of his surgical gown. Now that she was conscious, however, he helped her to her feet with a brusque motion, as if he couldn't wait to take his hands off her.

She leaned weakly against the side of the operating table, breathing deeply as her head gradually cleared. Dr. Sawyer stood watching her, arms folded across his chest.

"I—thank you very much for your help, Doctor." Finally Leslie turned to him, hardly daring to meet his eyes. "I'm sorry about this, and I can promise you it won't happen again."

"You can be sure of that," he stated firmly. "I intend to recommend you be dismissed at once. I should have done it the other day."

"Oh no, you can't do that! Please!"

"I can, and I will. I have a duty to this hospital, Miss Bennett. I can't endanger the lives of patients by allowing incompetent nurses to care for them."

Leslie's temper flared, just as it had at their first skirmish at the clinic. "Incompetent, am I? Then why did you ask me to become your regular assistant?"

She had scored a point, she knew, for a hint of uncertainty flashed across his features. "That was before—"

"Before you realized that *I* was your assistant—the notorious child abuser!" The words were out before Leslie could stop them. "Dr. Sawyer, you are narrow-minded and snobbish and . . . and judge and jury all at once!" She turned away and was astonished when his firm hand came down on her shoulder, wheeling her to face him. There was a disturbing gleam in those light eyes, as if he were enjoying this unexpected game of cat-and-mouse, and she found herself resisting his touch with all her remaining energy.

"That's not what I meant, and I think you know it," he said smoothly, but his fingers bit into her shoulder. "I started to say that I had asked you to assist me before I knew that you are subject to fainting spells."

"I've never fainted before," Leslie defended herself, "and the only reason I probably did today is because I've been ill and overworked." It was too late; she had said more than she intended. Would she *never* learn not to give this enemy more ammunition?

"Then you have even less reason to be on a hospital staff," Dr. Sawyer pointed out. "And I intend to inform the O.R. supervisor of that fact right now."

"But—"

"And let me assure you that I am not a complete ogre, despite your belief. I do not intend to blacken your character or to mention the pathetic state of your infant the last time I saw her. In short, you can be as careless as you like, Miss Bennett. . . ." He pulled her toward him, his face grim, "But not in this hospital, not with my patients. Is that clear?"

He was shaking her, and Leslie's anger burst its bounds. How dare he assume such terrible things about her? "You're the cruelest person I've ever met!" She pulled away from his grip and staggered against the table. "And you call yourself a healer!" Tears blurred her eyes, and she could feel the room starting to whirl again, the bite of nausea rising in her throat.

"Here, now . . ." His fingers were on her shoulder once more, but it was a gentler hand, a quieter voice that spoke. "Don't go getting faint again."

Instinctively Leslie flinched at his touch, and caught an

expression of remorse flitting across his firm features. He sighed, his anger apparently spent. "This has been a regrettable conversation, Miss Bennett. And I can't let you go in this distraught state. Take off your gown, get your things, and I'll drive you home."

Leslie straightened, gathering her shattered pride around her like a mantle. "That's not necessary, Doctor. I can—"

"No, you can't. You're in no condition to drive. Get going." His command brooked no argument, and Leslie was not up to it anyway. The quarrel had stolen not only her strength but her dignity. How could she have behaved so, shouting at a senior member of the hospital staff like that! And she had prided herself on her professionalism, her devotion to duty.

She bathed her face with cool water from the tap. She had been horrible, and she knew it. But there was something about Steven Sawyer that got under her skin. They had instinctively clashed at the clinic, and their dislike for one another had only intensified each time they met. In all her experience with men—and Leslie certainly didn't have much—she had never come up against such a domineering and rude man.

And yet he could certainly be kind when it suited him. She recalled his affectionate conversation with Mr. Parker, the warm appreciation he had given her in O.R. before she had fainted and spoiled his illusion. And the staff seemed to regard him with fondness, too. It was a puzzle.

Leslie dried her face, noticing again the bluish smudges under her eyes, and admitted for the first time that Dr. Sawyer had come to the only honest conclusion. "Lord, I've been wrong," she whispered. "I'm not well, am I? At least not strong enough to do my job the way it should be done and take care of Penny, too. I've tried to do the wrong thing for the right reason, and it didn't work. It never does, does it?" Perhaps if she had a few weeks to relax, gain weight, and find someone decent to care for Penny during the day . . . but there was no time. She had to have another job, and another paycheck, right away. "Lord," she murmured as she picked up her purse and headed for the corridor, "what am I going to *do*?"

4

*H*e was waiting for her near the main entrance, dressed in a navy blue business suit and white shirt open at the collar, a tie slung carelessly around his neck. His hands were thrust in his pockets, jingling coins, his toe tapping impatiently. Leslie looked for a moment at the well-shaped dark head, the tall leanness of his body, and a strange prickly sensation started in her toes. He was really handsome, perhaps the best-looking man she had ever known, and if he didn't have such a rotten disposition, if they had met under more honest circumstances . . .

Then Dr. Sawyer flicked a glance her way, and Leslie saw again the cynical expression she had already learned to dread, and the dream vanished. It was too late. He thought her something she was not, and she had been caught in her own duplicity. And yet she had no choice. For Penny's protection the masquerade must continue, no matter how much it might hurt.

Wordlessly, Dr. Sawyer put out his hand for her car keys as Leslie approached, and her grip tightened on her purse. "This really isn't necessary, Dr. Sawyer. And . . . and how will you get back to the hospital?"

"There *are* cabs, you know." His cool retort stung, but she had no stomach for another round of bickering. Surrendering, she placed the keys in his outstretched palm, and preceded him to the parking lot and her little Volkswagen.

"Interesting car," Steven commented, sliding behind

the wheel and releasing the seat as far back as it would go. "Looks like it needs a rest as much as you do."

Leslie refused to rise to the bait. Instead, she bit her lip and stared blindly out the window, willing the ride to be over soon.

There was an uncomfortable silence as the Volkswagen lurched along, and then Dr. Sawyer sighed. "Would you like to tell me where we're going?" he asked calmly.

"Oh, I'm sorry. I live just a few blocks past the street clinic."

"The clinic? That's a pretty rough neighborhood."

Why should you care? Leslie wanted to shout. But instead she shrugged. *Play it flippant, play it cool. Don't give him the satisfaction of knowing how he has ruined all your plans.*

"Up there," she pointed after several silent minutes had passed. "Just around the corner, the first house on the right."

He slid into a parking space and turned off the ignition. Ready to bolt, Leslie looked over at him, waiting for the return of her keys. Instead, he sat frowning at the run-down street.

"Cincinnati has so many nice areas. Why are you living here?" he asked. "Surely your salary could provide a better neighborhood."

"My *former* salary," she reminded him, and was perversely pleased to see him flush with embarrassment. "I needed to be close to the hospital while Penny was receiving treatment, and at the time I rented the rooms I had no job and very little money. Then there's the matter of baby-sitting fees, but these things aren't any of your concern, and—"

"Never mind." He held up a weary hand. "Get out, and I'll see you to your apartment."

Leslie froze. "Why? I'm certainly capable—"

"So you keep saying," he responded dryly. "But the next time you faint—in the hall or on the stairs—there may not be a doctor around."

Leslie gave in, knowing he was right. She hadn't eaten lunch, and the heat, kept at bay by the hospital air conditioning, was wrapping itself around her like a heavy blanket. But she didn't want him to see her pathetic rooms. Perhaps he would just accompany her to the front porch. . . .

She got out of the car, her damp uniform sticking to every inch of her, and started for the front steps, Dr. Sawyer following. But luck was not with her, for as she climbed to the dilapidated porch, Mrs. Briggs, her cranky landlady, flung open the door. "There you are," she announced peevishly. "Ten minutes late, and I'm missing the TV news—"

"Is Penny all right?" Leslie interrupted.

"Just fine, except she's awful cranky. I told you before, Mrs. Bennett, if she keeps fussing like that—"

Leslie brushed past her to the hall where Penny's bed had been set on the stained floor. "There's my sweetheart," she crooned softly, bending to lift Penny into her arms, "there's my little love." The baby was wet again.

"Just a minute—who're you and where. . . ?" Leslie heard Mrs. Briggs shouting, and was amazed when Dr. Sawyer strode into the dingy hallway. She had almost forgotten about him.

His now-familiar frown was back in place, and Leslie tensed. What now? "I need my pay, Mrs. Bennett," Mrs. Briggs was saying plaintively as she looked Steven up and down, not missing a detail of his immaculate appearance. "Now don't you go complaining again because I didn't bathe the baby—it's hard with them casts, and—"

"Never mind." Juggling Penny over one shoulder, Leslie fumbled in her purse for the folded bill and handed it to Mrs. Briggs, who was still eyeing the doctor with interest.

"He your husband?" she asked, grinning coyly.

"No!" Leslie gasped. "I . . . I told you my husband is dead, Mrs. Briggs."

"So you say," she leered, raising a scraggly eyebrow. "But I'll have no shenanigans going on in my boarding-house, understand? This is a respectable place, mind you, and—"

Leslie turned and bolted up the stairs. It was too much; she couldn't take any more. First Dr. Sawyer and his baiting, then a leering landlady—why did everyone think the worst of her? She fumbled for her key, pushed the door open, and deposited Penny gratefully on the sagging couch. First a tepid sponge bath for the baby, then her bottle, then—

"Where do you want these?" Steven's stiff voice came from the doorway. Leslie whirled around. He was standing with that same grim expression on his face, holding Penny's portable bed and diaper bag.

"What are you doing up here?" Leslie cried. "Didn't you hear my landlady? If she suspects that you . . . that I . . . I could get put out on the street!"

"I'll leave the door open so she can eavesdrop," he retorted, slamming the diaper bag on a nearby table.

"But . . . oh, what's the use? And you can't leave the door open; there's a drunk across the hall who—"

"Then I'll throw him down the stairs." He deposited the bed on the couch next to Penny and bent over her. "First I want to take a look at this poor little thing."

"Not now," Leslie objected. Would he never *leave*? "She's wet and needs her bath. Mrs. Briggs doesn't take very good care of her."

"Then why in heaven's name do you bring her to that . . . that slum downstairs?" He was undressing Penny, keeping his tone low so the baby wouldn't be frightened, but his disgust with the whole situation was evident.

Leslie felt her temper rising. "And what choice do I

have? No day-care center will take Penny until her casts are removed, and I have to work. She has to eat, doesn't she?" Her voice trembled dangerously. "Oh, why should I expect you to understand? You've probably never had a problem in your whole life!"

Dr. Sawyer smiled slowly, his eyes still intent on Penny. "I wouldn't be too sure of that if I were you."

"Well . . ." Leslie shrugged, remembering her vow to play it cool. She went to the small sink, ran water, and found the heavy towel that Penny lay on for her nightly sponge bath. Leslie took a bottle of formula from the small refrigerator, wiped the perspiration from her forehead, and turned to see Steven standing, hands on his hips, a puzzled frown on his face as he looked around the room. Leslie watched his gaze travel from her dismal windowsill herb garden, struggling for air in the oppressively hot apartment, to the tubes of Penny's salves near the sink, to the old Bible on the battered coffee table. Well, at least it was clean, an oasis of sparkling glass and furniture polish amid the surrounding desolation. Let him look, let him mock her attempts to create some order and peace out of the chaos.

He said nothing, and when the silence lengthened awkwardly, Leslie went to pick up Penny. "There's my little angel. It's time for your bath," she crooned, and Penny's fists waved in response. "Oh!" Leslie caught her breath. "Listen! She cooed—she really did!" She swung a delighted face to the doctor, and was shocked to meet an expression of hostility mixed with bewilderment. Without a word, he turned swiftly and strode out of the apartment, slamming the door behind him.

What on earth. . . ? But Leslie shrugged, too tired to even care what his latest display of temper was all about. At least he was gone, and she would never see him again. The thought echoed hollowly somewhere in the recesses of her mind, but she was past caring about anything but the jobs at hand. Bathe Penny, feed Penny, rock and sing Penny to sleep, then a shower for herself . . .

She was towel-drying her hair when she heard a knock on the door. "Go away," she called, firmness being the only thing her troublesome alcoholic neighbor understood.

"Open the door." It was Dr. Sawyer's voice.

Astonished, Leslie tied the sash of the thin robe around her waist, glanced despairingly in the mirror at her tangled hair, damp and curling around her flushed face, and crossed the room in bare feet. Perhaps he had forgotten something?

When she opened the door, Dr. Sawyer was standing in the hall, suit jacket slung over his shoulder and carrying two large bags that sent a mouth-watering aroma wafting toward her. "Have you had dinner yet?" he asked abruptly.

"Well, no, I . . ." She pushed back her unruly hair in surprise and confusion.

His gaze traveled across her freshly scrubbed face, the thin robe, and suddenly she knew—without knowing how she knew—that despite his calm demeanor, he was as ill at ease as she. Perhaps the food was a peace offering, a way to make up for the fact that he had had her dismissed. Leslie had been taught to forgive, and that included enemies as well as friends. "Come in," she said quietly. "I'll change, and—"

"No need for that. I'll be leaving soon. I have clinic duty tonight." Steven strode past her and deposited the bags on the coffee table. Leslie noticed that they were from Peterson's, an expensive restaurant near the hospital, one she had never been to. There was soup, covered dinner plates, and containers of coffee, rich and sweet-smelling. She watched, dazed, as Steven arranged everything, then looked up and caught her bemused gaze. He shrugged and smiled wryly. "As I told you, cabs are handy. Sit down before everything gets cold."

Feeling like a princess in the middle of a hovel, Leslie

obeyed. The soup was heavenly, thick with noodles and to-
matoes, warming her hollow stomach. She ate, not caring
that he was watching her, not even pausing to wonder why.
It wasn't until she was almost through with the main course,
a delightful steak-and-eggs combination, that Steven finally
spoke.

"You mentioned that you've been sick," he broached
the subject casually. "What sort of illness did you have?"

"An especially bad strain of flu," Leslie answered, but-
tering another roll and attempting to match his civil tone.
"I was hospitalized because of a high fever. Although," she
added defensively, "I was *not* contagious by the time I was
released."

"Of course. But coming on top of Penny's birth, an illness must have been quite difficult for you."

Leslie swallowed guiltily. "Well, yes, it was."

"And Penny? Did your family take care of her while
you were in the hospital?"

Her eyes clouded with pain. "I have no family," she
said, remembering her parents, her grandmother, Lee—all
of them gone.

"And you're not a widow?" Steven probed gently.

"No." At least on this point she could be completely
truthful. "I have never had a husband."

"I see. And you left . . . Minnesota, was it? . . . because . . ."

"Because of many reasons, none of which I care to discuss, and none that are related to my professional life."

Silence hung between them for a moment and Leslie
sensed, oddly, that he believed her, although she didn't see
why it mattered. He had judged her already and found her
guilty of . . . whatever the circumstances led him to believe.

Now Steven leaned back, put his arms behind his head,
and looked thoughtfully at the cracked ceiling. She could
see the dark crisp hair escaping from his open collar, the

outline of his muscular arms under the white shirt, and she felt again that peculiar sensation in her throat.

"I have an aunt, an elderly aunt," Steven began, still looking at the ceiling. "She raised me, and she still lives alone in our old family homestead in the Kentucky hill country, a few hours' drive from here. Cincinnati may be a thriving metropolis, but there's an entirely different culture just a short distance away, you know."

"No," Leslie answered, puzzled at the conversation's turn. "I didn't know."

"Anyway," Steven sighed, and she noticed the lines of weariness around his mouth, "Aunt Mae recently developed diabetes, and she's afraid of her daily insulin shot. I suspect that occasionally she skips it, and she doesn't follow a proper diet either. You know what effect that can have on a diabetic."

"Yes, of course." Leslie's mind was lingering on his first statement. "I didn't know you came from Kentucky. You . . . you don't have any accent."

Steven smiled wryly. "Well, several years at Harvard medical school did smooth out my speech," he explained. "But if you listen closely, you can still hear a trace of that hill country twang."

"You went to Harvard!" Leslie remarked. "That's quite an achievement."

"With a combination of loans, scholarships, grants— and plenty of part-time jobs," Steven answered. "Sometimes I didn't sleep for days. . . ." His eyes were misted with memories, and Leslie remembered her earlier jibes about his charmed snobbish lifestyle and felt ashamed. It couldn't have been easy for a poor country boy to fit into the rarified atmosphere of one of the wealthiest universities in the world.

"Getting back to Aunt Mae," he began again. "She's a terrible patient, cranky and stubborn. None of the housekeepers I've hired have stayed longer than a month. Of course, there are only a few neighbors, the house is isolated and very run down . . . Aunt Mae just won't take an interest in anything anymore."

Leslie cleared her throat. "This is all very interesting, Dr. Sawyer, but why—"

"Because," he looked at her for the first time with that intent blue gaze, "I'm wondering if you'd take the job."

"What?" Leslie's mouth fell open in astonishment.

"The job of housekeeper. Not that there'd be that much physical labor involved—a high-school girl from town comes in every day to clean, now that summer vacation has started. But you'd have to do the errands, supervise Aunt Mae's diet and medication, and be a companion to her, if you could tolerate her poor temper."

"It's probably a family trait," Leslie said without thinking, then bit her lip. "I'm sorry. I guess I'm just so surprised—"

"It would be a good solution for you," Steven went on as if he hadn't heard. "Country living will certainly restore your own health, and you'd have more time for Penny. The job's temporary, just until I can convince Aunt Mae to move into Cincinnati where I can keep a closer eye on her. Oh, and there's a salary in addition to your board." He named a figure which was more than half of what she had been earning at the hospital. Without rent, food, or day-care payments, it seemed a magnificent sum.

Leslie's head reeled. Why was he making this offer? Was he *that* desperate? "You . . . you don't even know me," she murmured. "How can you entrust your sick aunt to a total stranger?"

"Well," Steven smiled wryly again, "that's a fair question, considering our . . . previous difficulties. I'm a Christian, Miss Bennett, and Christians are supposed to be just. Although you're physically run down at the moment, you *are* a competent nurse—I saw that for myself today in surgery. I like the way you handle patients, too. I know you would take good care of Aunt Mae.

"And then there's your daughter." He paused, apparently searching for the right words. "You could have simply taken the so-called easy route and had an abortion. Many girls in your situation would do just that. But you chose to give life to Penny. I admire that. I believe that was the right decision. Having a baby without being married isn't an unusual thing today, but it still must have required a lot of courage."

Leslie flushed. Although she agreed wholeheartedly with his views on abortion, the last thing she wanted was a discussion on her presumed unwed-mother status. What would Dr. Sawyer say if he knew the whole truth?

"Finally," Steven continued, "although Penny's condition was appalling the first time I saw her, she's improved dramatically. You've cared well for her these past weeks under difficult circumstances. Which means—at least temporarily—that you've put her welfare ahead of yours."

"What . . . what do you mean, temporarily?" A warning bell sounded in Leslie's mind.

"I mean, I'm not fooled by your air of innocence, by those big brown eyes that can turn the tears on and off at will." Steven's tone was matter-of-fact. But, dismayed, Leslie saw again the enemy that she thought had been banished. "I've met women like you before, and sooner or later, whenever you've recovered, you're probably going to return to the kind of lifestyle that got you into this mess in the first place."

"Women like me?" Leslie's mouth dropped. "How dare you!"

"Don't worry." Steven narrowed his eyes. "Your character is of no concern to me, *Mrs.* Bennett, provided you care well for my aunt."

Leslie was on her feet, shaking as if from a physical assault. "Get out," she murmured through clenched teeth. "Get out before I . . . I . . ."

She looked around for something heavy to fling at him—oh, the satisfaction of venting her rage!—but Steven was getting to his feet, too, and she had to put an end to it. Whirling, she bolted for the bathroom and slammed the door, securing the lock with trembling fingers. Through the sound of her jagged gasps, she heard his heavy tread on the bare floor, then the sound of the apartment door closing behind him.

———

She slept fitfully, waking to weep quietly, then drifting off into uneasy slumber again. As usual, she dreamed of Gram, of Lee. . . . Part of the dream also encompassed two shadowy figures, one gently bending over her bed, the other laughingly tossing her in the air like a doll. She could not see them clearly, but she knew they were her parents. How different her life might have been had they lived!

As always in the dream, she walked and talked with her family, was comforted by their companionship—and awakened to dried tears on her cheeks and the knowledge that she was alone.

Not really alone, though, for as she roused herself wearily again, the weak light of dawn outlined Penny, sleeping softly in her little bed. Penny was hers now, no matter what, and she would not let the cruel assumptions of others turn her away from this commitment.

And yet—Leslie bit her lip as a quiver ran through her—she hadn't expected it to be so painful. The sacrifice and fatigue she would gladly endure, but would she ever be able to forget Dr. Sawyer's taunting cruelty, the way he had pretended to be decent and concerned for her welfare, only to shatter her budding hopes with his demeaning assumptions? More than the loss of a possible job, Leslie mourned the spitefulness that had leaped between them from the start, a bitter barrier that could never be surmounted.

At times she wondered what might have happened if she had been honest with Steven from the start, and perhaps enlisted his aid in trying to straighten out the mess she'd gotten into. But, no, he had called himself a "just man," but justice without mercy could be deadly. From what she had observed of him so far, she assumed Steven would have no compassion for her.

"My dear Miss Bennett, you're a lawbreaker, a child-snatcher," she could almost hear him saying in that remote, disdainful tone. "I cannot have a fugitive from justice working on my staff. The child must go back to the Chicago authorities immediately. Her father has a legal right to decide her future, even if he is in prison." She could hear him laugh contemptuously at her blundering, not understanding that she had acted out of love, however misguided. What could he know of tenderness and concern for those weaker than himself? Although mistaken, he had thought Leslie courageous to refuse an abortion, but his respect and solicitude stopped short when he confronted the *results* of that decision. No, Steven Sawyer would never be a refuge, not for her or Penny, perhaps not for anyone.

She brushed a lingering tear aside, and reached over to the nightstand for a tissue. Her fingers touched Gram's old Bible and she held it close to her, as she had done so often before sending it to Lee. How glad she was that Lee had it with her at the end.

Lee . . . she thought about her sister with the familiar ache of frustrated affection. How could Gram have raised them both in the same way, and have them turn out so different from each other? Her twin had been wild and mercurial, chafing at restrictions and scoffing at "all that religious stuff." And she was easygoing and dependable Leslie, who'd found her faith in God to be joyful and freeing, empowering her to be more than she ever thought she could be.

"You will know the truth, and the truth will set you free." And so it had. Despite the burdens of school, the hardship of occasional loneliness and confusion, there had always been Jesus Christ, the loving source of her strength, the wellspring of her vitality. And yet . . . the thought plagued her. She was not living the truth now. She would never forsake her Lord, but she *was* abandoning one of the Bible's tenets, the belief that truth should always prevail. She had started on the wrong path back in that Chicago tenement, and the lie had grown heavier, more pervasive until it tainted every action she took. But to make a clean start of it all, to send Penny back to a foster home or worse, to a sordid life with her father—she couldn't do that. It took more faith than Leslie had to believe that was the best solution.

The reality of the situation soon broke into her reverie. This morning she would have to begin the difficult task of job-hunting again. Hospitals were out; if she knew Steven Sawyer, he would refuse to give her a decent reference to any medical facility. It would have to be something else. She put the Bible back on the table, noticing absently that its back lining was torn. Vowing to mend it sometime, she reached for yesterday's newspaper and ran her eye down the Classifieds. Art teacher, cafe waitress, clerical worker . . . not much from which to choose.

Well, she would worry about it later. Right now, Penny was moving around in her bed, making little "feed-me" sounds, and Leslie had to get dressed and go to the hospital to collect her final paycheck before starting to look for a new job.

An hour later Leslie knocked on Mrs. Briggs' door and handed the baby to her. "I'll be home early today, Mrs.

Briggs," she began, but the landlady held up a white envelope.

"Came in the mail for you yesterday," she sniffed. "Clean forgot to give it to you last night, with the gentleman and all. . . ."

Leslie eyed the envelope. It had a Chicago postmark, probably Penny's birth certificate. She felt a warm glow of gratitude; the little friend of Lee's had helped her after all.

"And I've decided that I'm not going to be able to keep the baby anymore, Mrs. Bennett, and that's a fact." Mrs. Briggs' whining voice finally penetrated.

"What?" Leslie cried. "But, Mrs. Briggs, you know I can't take Penny to a day-care center yet. What will we do?"

The landlady shrugged. "Not my concern. Oh," she relented, seeing Leslie's stricken face, "I'll take her today, but that's the end of it. She just cries too much, that's all."

Penny let out a contented coo, the result of a full stomach and a powdered bottom, and Mrs. Briggs had the grace to look guilty. Leslie flung her a despairing glance and ran down the porch stairs. Now what? She slid behind the wheel of the Volkswagen. No baby-sitter, no job . . .

She still held the letter and now slit it open quickly, surprised to see two rumpled sheets of paper instead of the photocopy she had expected. It was a letter from Sandy, the little teenager, and despite smudges and misspelled words, the message was clear—and ominous.

> Tony broke out of jail and came here. He says you have something he wants, and he means to get it. You better run. Tony doesn't know where you are, but he'll find out. And he can be awful mean.

The prickly sensation of fear started in the back of Leslie's neck and spread, encompassing every part of her. Somehow, Tony was free, and it wouldn't take him long to locate her, not if he knew she was a nurse, which Lee surely would have told him. Tracing Leslie through hospitals or nurses' associations would be time-consuming, but she remembered the tough, determined-looking expression in the photo Lee had sent, and knew Tony would be equal to the task.

Leslie definitely had something he wanted—his baby daughter. The image of the Chicago tenement rose before her eyes, and her hands tightened on the wheel. No! With every bit of strength she possessed, she would keep that from happening. She would run, right now. She would pack everything up, grab Penny, and go. But where? With no job, no home, where could she and the baby be safe? Would she have to keep running forever?

And then, almost through a mist, she heard the voice of Steven Sawyer. *"There are few neighbors . . . the house is in an isolated setting. . . ."* A vision of a rustic sanctuary rose before her eyes, a quiet hideaway where no one would ever find them.

But it was insane! To approach Steven again, after all that had happened between them, to humble herself before his merciless stare, to beg for help after all she had said—and perhaps to be turned away?

She couldn't do it. And yet, what choice did she have?

"For Penny," she murmured finally. "Only for Penny." She started the engine and turned the car toward the hospital.

5

*I*f she lived to be a hundred, Leslie ruefully admitted later, she would never forget that confrontation in Steven's office, the moment when she staked everything on the chance for freedom—and won.

She had tiptoed into the small suite of ground-floor cubbyholes where the staff surgeons interviewed their patients. As she entered she prayed fervently that she would not have to announce herself to a curious receptionist, or brave a crowd of onlookers in the waiting room, should Steven loudly banish her from his lofty presence. Her prayers were answered, for the suite was deserted except for voices coming from behind the door marked "Steven Sawyer, M.D." Fortunately he had only one patient, and while Leslie waited for the visit to come to an end, she could practice several approaches, one of which might thaw Dr. Sawyer's icy heart—if he in fact *had* a heart, which she sincerely doubted.

"Dr. Sawyer, I have considered your kind offer, and . . ." Ridiculous. It wasn't meant in kindness, and they both knew it.

Well, then, how about: "The baby and I desperately need a place to stay, and . . ." Wrong. That was true, but that would also let him know just how frightened and upset she was, and he wouldn't hesitate to turn the screws, enjoying her predicament.

Leslie sighed, impatient at her own ineptness when it

came to men. Why hadn't she developed the so-called feminine wiles that seemed second nature to most women? While her counterparts had been learning to flirt and wind boyfriends around their little fingers, she'd had her nose in a book. This wasn't the first time she wished she had just a small part of Lee's wild ways—her sister would have had Steven Sawyer eating out of her hand within five minutes of meeting him.

While Leslie sat frowning in concentration, however, the conversation behind Steven's door had grown louder, and she belatedly realized that the other person was a woman, an angry woman from the sound of it. Did Steven fight with every female he knew?

"And if you think that I enjoy waiting at a party until all hours for you—"

"I came as soon as I could. You knew last night was my clinic duty." In comparison to the woman's strident tones, Steven sounded almost reasonable.

"Oh yes, your street people, and the time they take away from real patients . . ."

"Street people are *real* patients too. And if I'm to stay on in Cincinnati—"

"What do you mean, if?"

Flustered, Leslie looked for a place to hide. It was bad enough to eavesdrop on an obviously private conversation, but to be caught at it when she was about to throw herself on Steven's doubtful mercies . . .

"Rita, calm down and listen to me." It was too late. Steven's office door crashed open, and a statuesque blonde stalked out, her perfectly molded face set in a pout. Everything about her spoke of being handmade, expensive, and chic. Dazzled, Leslie could only stare at the silk dress, the long, graceful legs, as the woman clicked past her and out the door. So that was the exquisite and spoiled Rita Marchand, Steven's probable fiancée.

"Well, this is certainly turning into an interesting day," Steven's sardonic voice sounded behind her, and Leslie turned to see him leaning against the doorjamb, arms folded across his chest in the now-familiar pose. "To what do I owe the pleasure of *your* company?"

"I got to thinking about that job with your Aunt Mae." Leslie forgot her rehearsed speech. "I decided to take it."

"Oh, really? A sudden change of heart?" She caught the amusement in his light eyes and lifted her chin.

"You could call it that. I'll accept, on one condition."

"Really, Miss Bennett, you intrigue me. What is the condition?"

"That . . ." Leslie's heart was racing despite her controlled demeanor, and she heard her own firm statement as if a stranger spoke. "That you promise to stay away from your aunt's house while I'm there."

"I . . . see." Steven appeared taken aback at her words. "And you really think I would abandon my aunt to you without a backward glance?"

"You could safely do so. I would take good care of her."

"No doubt." Steven's eyes narrowed. "But I'm curious. What is your real reason for wanting me out of the picture, Miss Bennett? Do I know too much about your doubtful background? Are you afraid I would tell Aunt Mae that your 'little innocent girl' routine is only a pose?"

He had pushed her too far. "I will tell you why, since you press the issue." Calmly Leslie aimed every word like a dart. "Because you are the most hateful, unkind man I have ever had the misfortune to meet. You harass and mock me at every turn—and enjoy it. I wouldn't have a moment's peace, much less the energy to nurse your aunt, if I had to deal with you, too."

Steven's aggression had faded at her words, to be replaced by—could it possibly be—disappointment? Whatever answer he had expected, he definitely didn't receive it.

They stared at each other for an uncomfortable moment. "Well," Steven said finally, "I can't accept your condition. I check on Aunt Mae regularly, I always have, and I'll continue to do so, no matter who is nursing her."

Leslie's shoulders sagged. She had lost. "All right. Then I guess there's nothing more to say, is there?"

"No." It was the final curt rejection, and she fumbled for her purse, barely able to see through the haze of disappointment that came over her. Then Steven spoke again, almost casually.

"Actually, I could promise you one thing."

"Oh?" She froze, daring to hope once again.

"Yes. On my visits out to the farm, since I'm so disgusting to you, I could promise to avoid you as much as possible. Would that be enough for your sensitive little psyche?"

"Oh . . . oh yes!" A second chance! She swung shining eyes to him, and saw in surprise the dull flush that had darkened his cheeks. If she had known him better, she would have thought he was nervous—or even a bit ashamed?

The illusion quickly passed. "Be ready tomorrow at five p.m.," Steven said shortly, turning toward his office. "I'll pick you up."

"But I can drive myself."

"Don't argue. The sooner I settle you in with Aunt Mae, the sooner I can get on with my own affairs." He shot her a withering look. "Not that you would notice or care, Miss Bennett, but I do have a lot on my mind."

"I did notice, and she's very beautiful." Overwhelmed with relief, Leslie gathered her belongings, feeling suddenly magnanimous. "I wish you both the best, Dr. Sawyer. I really do."

"Don't be ridiculous," he said and turned away.

What was ridiculous about wishing Steven a happy life with his fiancée? Leslie didn't know, and now, scrunched into the passenger side of her Volkswagen, she really didn't care. The man maneuvering her little car in and out of rush-hour traffic was an enigma wrapped in mystery, and with any luck, by tomorrow he would almost be completely out of her life. From the corner of her eye she saw the tautness of his narrow fingers on the steering wheel, and sensed the tension of controlled muscles and set jaw—did he never relax? Well, it was not her concern if he chose to live his life in such a driven style.

Not that Leslie would have admitted it to him for a moment, but she *was* relieved that he had insisted on driving her to Aunt Mae's. They were out of Cincinnati now and onto the ribbon of highway that had already become Kentucky. The heat was still intense, and she would have had her hands full driving, following directions, and caring for Penny if she fussed along the way.

Comforted by a full tummy and the rocking motion of the drive, the baby had already slipped into slumber in her car seat. It might have been a halfway decent journey after all—that is, if the strain between them hadn't been so obvious.

They had spoken to each other only once, when Steven had arrived at her boardinghouse room and looked disbelievingly at the few boxes piled on the floor. "This is all you're bringing?" he asked without even a greeting first.

"This is all I've got," Leslie explained, observing his jeans and T-shirt. She had never seen Steven in casual clothes and they made him look, somehow, more human. Her dislike for him, however, hadn't diminished.

"Why are you wearing a uniform?" he asked bluntly. "A farm isn't the place for professional clothes. Don't you have any common sense at all?"

"You never told me—" Leslie stopped. He was right,

jeans would have been far more appropriate for a long drive and rural life. But she had wanted to make a good impression on his aunt. And how was Leslie to know what would be acceptable to her elderly patient? "Oh, stop criticizing me!" she had countered, color rising to her cheeks. "I thought you promised to leave me alone!"

Steven swung a box onto his shoulder. "It'll be a pleasure," he had muttered as he stomped down the stairs.

Now, however, as the miles passed, Leslie could feel herself relaxing. There was something soothing about the lush, bluish colored landscape, broken by bluffs or an occasional rail-fenced farm, ringed with distant hills that seemed to melt into the horizon. "I've never been to Kentucky," she remarked. "It looks lovely."

"It's a nice place to live." Steven, also apparently lulled by the serene atmosphere, answered her almost pleasantly. "Its name comes from a Native American word meaning 'Land where we will live tomorrow.' "

"That's beautiful."

"Kentucky's mostly rural—our farm grows corn. And of course horses are a big industry, too."

"Yes, I've seen the Kentucky Derby and the Lexington horse shows on television."

"The people here are hospitable and easygoing, although they do spin plenty of tall tales and never back down from a fight. But they're loyal and kind, and I think you'll like them very much."

"I hope your Aunt Mae likes *me* . . . and Penny," Leslie sighed, voicing a question she'd been worrying about. Aunt Mae sounded like a difficult patient. How would she react to Leslie's unorthodox situation?

"I've told her you're a widow if that's what's bothering you." Steven seemed to read her mind. "It's the simplest way, isn't it? I certainly don't expect you to accomplish anything more than the basics with Aunt Mae, and you probably won't get to know her well anyway since you won't be on the job that long."

Even now it seemed he could hardly wait to be rid of her. He must be counting the days until his aunt would agree to move to Cincinnati.

"It must be hard to think of selling your farm," she said casually. "After all, you grew up there, didn't you?"

"Aunt Mae and my father grew up there, too," Steven answered. "Aunt Mae became a teacher in the town school. My father farmed the land and got married, and eventually they had me. Yes, I was raised there, and when my folks suddenly died, Aunt Mae completed the job."

"They died together?"

"Yes, when I was fourteen." Steven's fingers tightened slightly on the steering wheel. "They died of pneumonia, within one day of each other."

"Of pneumonia?" Leslie was incredulous. "But that's easily cured with antibiotics, or in the hospital."

"Only if a doctor can provide the necessary treatment. In their case, he couldn't. He was stuck forty miles to the south in a freak blizzard. He didn't even get my call until it was too late."

"Why didn't another doctor come?"

"There were no other doctors. Our one and only clinic was almost twenty miles from home. Serious hospital cases had to go to the nearest big city, and that was quite a distance."

"But . . . but that's medieval!" Leslie was astonished. "How can people live without adequate health care?"

"Rural and mountain folks manage," Steven said. "They have no choice. I'm sure you know that although there's really not a shortage of physicians in the United States now, most of us choose to practice in metropolitan areas."

"Yes. I . . . I hadn't realized . . ." She thought again of

Steven's parents, of their needless deaths. "Wasn't your Aunt Mae able to help your parents?" she asked.

"She was snowed in by the same storm at school for three days," Steven answered slowly. "I was the only one home."

"You?" The tragic words gripped Leslie's heart. "You were with them through . . . through all of it?"

"With them, and utterly useless." His voice was suddenly harsh. "There was nothing I could do, nothing at all. I think that's one of the reasons I later decided to become a doctor. I never wanted to be so helpless again in the face of suffering."

"Oh, Steven, I'm so sorry." Tears welled up in her eyes, and impulsively she laid a hand on his sleeve. Startled, he turned to look at her, and for a brief moment she glimpsed a grieving fourteen-year-old boy looking out of his eyes. Then the smooth mask of detachment slid across his features once again. "It all happened a long time ago, Miss Bennett," he said in a tone reserved for a stranger. "I don't know why I mentioned it; it really shouldn't concern you at all."

"No, of course not." Awkwardly, she stifled the rejected sympathy, clasped her hands firmly on her lap, and stared out the window as silence once again descended.

The curving, rolling landscape slid past, and soon Steven turned into a rutted driveway. "Almost there," he remarked and Leslie leaned forward, eager for her first glimpse of her new home.

The house sat in a little cup of hills, half-hidden by foliage growing wildly right up to the road. Behind it stretched fields holding a well-tended corn crop, but the driveway they were traveling was rough, with loose gravel and sudden dips. Leslie looked at the broken stonework, the dilapidated outbuildings, the overgrown weeping willows sweeping green skirts across the shaggy grass. The house itself was a wandering stone and frame structure, three stories high, with a sagging front porch needing several coats of paint. From an upstairs window, a faded blue curtain blew in the breeze, like someone waving. The whole effect was one of benign charm. She loved it immediately.

Steven, however, did not share her enthusiasm. Pulling the car into a gravel clearing in front of the porch, he switched off the engine, looked around, and sighed. "If you think this is bad, wait until you see the inside," he muttered.

"It's not bad at all—" Leslie started to protest but was interrupted by the slam of the sagging screen door and a chubby figure coming eagerly down the steps.

"Hi, Dr. Steve! Welcome home!"

"Thanks, Dotty. It's good to be back." Steven smiled affectionately at her. The teenage girl, Leslie now realized, was wearing her hair in braids and an apron around her jeans. "This is Leslie Bennett, Aunt Mae's new nurse. Show her the ropes, will you?"

Dotty grinned and stuck a friendly hand through the car window. "Pleased to meet you, Miz Bennett. Can I help you carry anything in?"

"I'll get everything later, Dotty, thanks." Steven climbed out of the car and Leslie followed. "By the way," he asked, "how come you're still here, Dotty? Isn't it awfully late?"

"When I heard you were coming, I decided to stay and cook dinner for you," Dotty answered proudly. "I figured you'd be hungry."

"Dinner?" A dismayed expression crossed Steven's face, to be instantly replaced by one of politeness. "Well . . . that's certainly nice of you." He turned toward the house.

"And I wanted to see the baby, too," Dotty grinned at Leslie. "Can I?"

"Oh yes, of course." Pleased at the girl's warm welcome, Leslie carefully lifted the car seat from the backseat.

"Why don't you carry her into the house? I'll get her things."

"Oh, could I?" Dotty's freckled face beamed as Leslie laid the still-sleeping Penny in her arms. Dotty bent over the baby, lips parted in a fascinated smile. "She's so small."

"But heavy. Her casts weigh a ton." Leslie picked up the car seat and followed Dotty across the lawn and up the porch stairs. Stepping inside, she paused for a moment to look at the house that was now her refuge. A wide hallway, bare except for a battered table and lamp. To the left was an open archway with the living room beyond—large and well-lighted by high windows, but as sterile as the hallway. Past the living room was a dining area, including a magnificent hutch but completed by an unattractive table now set for dinner.

To Leslie's right was a closed door, probably a second parlor, and in front of her a curved staircase. The hall continued into the back of the house where the kitchen probably lay. Although the rooms were spacious, there seemed no hominess about them; no plants or accessories warmed the atmosphere. Everything she saw projected an attitude of indifference, as if no one had cared in a long, long time.

"Seen enough?" Steven was beside her, again sensing her reaction. "Want to resign?"

She threw him an indignant glance. "Of course not."

"Then come and meet Aunt Mae." He took her arm. "Dotty will see to the baby and, unfortunately," he sighed again, "the dinner."

Aunt Mae was sitting in a worn, oversized armchair that dwarfed her small round figure. Masses of snowy hair curled around a rosy face that, Leslie suspected, would normally be creased in a dimpled smile. At the moment, however, Aunt Mae wore a petulant expression traced with a tension common to patients who've recently received a difficult diagnosis. Far from acknowledging her situation, however, Aunt Mae seemed determined to ignore it.

"I'm sorry you came all this way for nothing, Mrs. Bennett," she said, taking Leslie's hand in an unexpectedly firm grip, "but as I continue to tell Steven, I really don't need any special care. Dotty and I manage just fine."

Suddenly there was a crash from the kitchen, followed by a muffled cry.

"Just fine, hmmm?" Steven spoke almost teasingly from the fireplace mantel where he leaned, hands in his pockets, watching the little scene with interest.

Aunt Mae met his eye with a muted but unmistakable twinkle. "All right, I admit she isn't a gourmet cook, but . . ."

"That will be one of Mrs. Bennett's jobs," Steven went on smoothly. "Wouldn't you like to have food that tastes like food, Aunt Mae?"

"Mrs. Bennett is a nurse, not a chef, Steven. Her training would be wasted here." Aunt Mae turned to Leslie. "My dear, I do appreciate your good intentions, but . . ."

"And I appreciate yours." Suddenly Leslie saw a possibility, and plunged ahead. "It can't be easy for someone like you—used to peace and quiet—to allow a baby into your home."

Aunt Mae looked momentarily bewildered. "The baby? Oh yes, I'd forgotten about her."

"I'm afraid you're welcoming two of the 'walking wounded' into your household, Miss Sawyer," Leslie went on quickly. "Between my recent illness and the baby's casts, well, I can't tell you what it means to us to be able to come here."

"Just temporarily, of course," Steven interjected casually from the fireplace.

"Oh yes," Leslie picked up his cue. "Just until we get on our feet again."

A perplexed frown flitted across Aunt Mae's brow, and

Leslie could see that she had measured the older woman correctly. Aunt Mae obviously hated the idea of needing care. But being asked to provide it for someone else touched the innate generosity of spirit Leslie had sensed in her. "Well . . ." Aunt Mae began.

"Dinner is served!" a flushed Dotty announced from the dining room doorway.

"Might as well get it over with," Steven murmured and went to help his aunt out of her chair. As he passed Leslie, he actually smiled at her, a *real* smile, without a hint of sarcasm or mockery. Something nice had happened to Steven since they had entered this quiet country place, Leslie realized. The thought warmed her right down to her toes.

Dotty's dinner was, perhaps, the most disastrous meal Leslie had ever endured. The food was poorly cooked, almost unidentifiable and, Leslie suspected, probably contained items unsuitable for a diabetic. Now she understood Steven's wry apprehension, but it was too late to decline, so good manners demanded that she at least make an attempt to eat. Chewing doggedly, she looked up once to find Steven watching her, amusement dancing in his light eyes as he silently acknowledged their shared misfortune. Aunt Mae, at the end of the table, seemed deep in thought and did little more than pick at her servings. Dotty ate with relish, oblivious to the others' reactions.

When the silence became uncomfortable, Leslie tried to begin a conversation. "That's a beautiful hutch, Miss Sawyer," she ventured. "I've never seen one quite so grand."

Aunt Mae looked fondly at the massive piece. "Steven's mother bought that at a farm sale and refinished it many years ago," she explained. "Restoring furniture was her hobby. She worked in the attic rooms—I imagine there are still plenty of good pieces up there."

"I'll have to clean that attic out one of these days,"

Steven remarked, casually burying a portion of his meat under a wilted lettuce leaf.

"There's no hurry, dear," Aunt Mae looked at him. "After all, I'm not going anywhere."

Steven cocked an eyebrow. "Cincinnati could be a nice place to live."

"Not for me."

Silence fell again, and Steven, having hidden as much dinner as possible under the lettuce, put his silverware down and stretched. "Think I'll wander around on the hills for a while, Aunt Mae."

His aunt looked up again, an innocent expression on her face. "The Ellis boy has a bad ear infection, I hear."

"Oh?"

"Wouldn't hurt to drop in on them, would it?"

Steven smiled, obviously familiar with her tactics. "The Ellises live in town, Aunt Mae. And I'm not driving Mrs. Bennett's Volkswagen another foot. It's about ready to collapse."

"You could toss Dotty's bicycle in the pickup truck and take her home on your way in."

Dotty, who had been following the exchange as if she'd heard it all before, chimed in on cue. "Oh, that would be great, Dr. Steve."

"What is this, a conspiracy?" Steven got up from the table in mock defeat. "Okay, Dotty, come on."

"See you all tomorrow!" Dotty tore off her apron and clattered out the front door behind Steven. Aunt Mae watched them go, then turned to Leslie.

"I'm not very subtle, am I?" she asked.

"I gather there's a shortage of physicians here," Leslie said.

"We're desperate. Steven never made a commitment to us, but we all had hoped that when he finished his residency . . ." She closed her lips firmly, but not before Leslie saw them tremble slightly.

"He . . . he seems to be a different person here," Leslie began cautiously. "More relaxed and lighthearted."

"Oh, he tries to pretend that he's outgrown us," Aunt Mae sighed. "But he can't fool me. His heart is in the hills, and it always will be."

"Then why—" Leslie began, but was interrupted by a thin wail from the living room. Hastily she went in and lifted Penny into her arms. "Wet again, little one, and all set to cry awhile." She looked apologetically at Aunt Mae. "Penny usually fusses a bit every evening before her night bottle. I hope it isn't going to bother you too much."

"Well, I'm not sure . . ." Aunt Mae frowned again, and Leslie realized with a sinking heart that nothing had really been settled between them. She could easily find herself homeless again, and then what would she do? With shaking fingers she changed Penny's diaper, then looked up in surprise to see that Aunt Mae was bending over her shoulder.

"A strong pair of lungs," the older woman observed, her eyes fastened intently on Penny's red face and waving fists.

"Very strong," Leslie said over the din. "But once she has her night bottle . . ."

"She sleeps until morning?"

"Well, no." Aunt Mae might as well be prepared. "She's up again at two, and then again around dawn."

"Gracious, child, no wonder you look so peaky!" Tact, obviously, was not one of Aunt Mae's strong points. But a gruff compassion was, for she briskly seated herself in the old rocker near the hearth and held out her arms. "As long as she's going to make all that noise, she might as well do it with me. You load the dishwasher, Mrs. Bennett, and then go up to bed. Your room's the first door on the right."

Leslie's mouth fell open. "You mean—"

"When Steven comes back, I'll have him bring his old crib down from the attic and put it into the room next to yours. No sense in it going to waste. Besides, that portable bed's no place for a growing child—much too small. And she ought to have some cereal in the evening, too, did you think of that? It would help her sleep a longer stretch."

A glow of gratitude warmed Leslie's heart as she meekly set the baby into Aunt Mae's open arms. "I'll feed her when I've done the dishes," she began, but the older woman silenced her with a formidable look.

"I'm quite capable of feeding a baby, young lady, despite my advanced age. *You* will go to bed."

Their eyes met over the baby's downy red hair, and a look of affectionate understanding passed between them. "Yes, ma'am," Leslie smiled softly.

"Call me Aunt Mae," the older woman commanded. "And bring a bottle of formula on your way upstairs."

Dotty had left the kitchen in an appalling state; spilled food and burned pans were everywhere. But Leslie tackled the cleanup with gusto, her heart singing. It was like a miracle, she reflected, and then realized with a start that it *was* a miracle. Somehow the Lord, in His infinite goodness, had lifted her from the pit of despair to the brink of hope. She and Penny would be safe from Tony, she knew. She would work hard to give Aunt Mae the best possible care, and Steven? Yes, someday Steven would be glad he had brought her here.

Later, as she prepared for bed in the large upstairs room and heard the first distant roll of thunder, she thought again of Steven, of the amusement they'd shared at dinner, far removed from their usual hostility. Perhaps . . . perhaps . . . but reality intruded, bringing her back to earth with a thump. How could she build a life, any kind of life, on a foundation of lies?

"Oh, Lord, help me," she prayed, kneeling against the bed in the solitude of her new room. "I feel so guilty. I'm lying to everyone and going against your will. But what else can I do?"

6

"*T*ake care of Penny," Lee was urgently calling to her. "Don't let Tony find her."

"Lee, Lee, don't go away!" Leslie tried to find her twin through the pounding blackness, but she could see nothing, and the familiar helplessness seized her. "Wait for me, I'm coming. . . ."

Suddenly Tony's bulky figure loomed in front of her, his arms open as he came toward her, and she shrank back. "No," she choked, hardly able to breathe. "No, Tony, please . . ." She tried to run but the noise and the darkness were all around her, and her legs wouldn't move. She gasped for air, unable to fill her lungs, but the silent Tony had reached her and she felt herself being pulled back, her way of escape barred. She wept, trying desperately to twist away, to free herself from his punishing grasp. "No, Tony, don't—"

"Leslie, Leslie, wake up! Leslie, you're having a nightmare."

Slowly the words worked their way into her consciousness, and her eyes opened. She was in the bedroom in Aunt Mae's house. The intangible nameless dread surrounded her, consuming her, but Steven was there, too, holding her firmly against his hard chest, murmuring words she couldn't hear.

"No!" she gasped as terror once again threatened to overwhelm her.

"It's a dream, Leslie, only a dream," Steven whispered. "You're safe now."

She stared at the outline of his face in incredulous relief as awareness slowly dawned. She was safe. A thunderstorm was raging outside, lighting the dark room with occasional bursts of brilliance, but she was safe. Abruptly, she dropped her face into her hands, a flood of tears spilling from her eyes, as Steven gathered her against him again. "Hush now," he whispered. His fingers moved to the back of her neck, slowly stroking her hair, soothing her until the sobbing and the desperate tension left her at last.

With a shuddering sigh she raised her face to his. "Steven," she sighed. "Thank you for . . . for being here."

Steven let her go and flicked on the bedside lamp. Its glow warmed the room and banished the last of her terrors. She was safe. Steven had said so.

"You were screaming," he said, matter-of-fact now that the crisis had passed. "I heard you in my room, all the way down the hall. I'm surprised you didn't wake Aunt Mae or the baby."

"I'm sorry," she whispered. "I . . . I have these dreams, and there doesn't seem to be anything I can do about them. . . ." Her voice trailed away.

"It's been rough on you, hasn't it?" Steven asked finally.

She was flustered. "Does it show?"

"Yes," he said quietly. "It shows."

There was something sad in the thin line of his mouth, and the way his eyes remained somber despite the gentle words. Bewildered, she felt the familiar animosity growing between them again, and longed somehow to banish it, to regain the closeness they had just shared. But Steven's next comment put an end to her hopes.

"Lee and Tony and how many others?" he asked, his voice suddenly hard. "No wonder you've made such a mess of your life."

His words were like an unexpected splash of cold water, but Leslie kept control even as her heart sank. "You have no right to judge me," she said quietly.

"No, I don't." Steven stood and looked down at her. "But I think it's safe to assume that Tony is Penny's father. Isn't he?"

She nodded, not trusting herself to speak.

Steven sighed, and she heard the regret in his words. "He's obviously hurt you badly, Leslie, and I'm sorry for you. But people who violate the rules do get hurt. You understand that, don't you?"

"It's you who doesn't understand," she murmured.

Steven was at the door now, and they looked at each other sadly across a chasm that neither of them could bridge. She felt the hopelessness even as she lifted her chin in a gesture of dignity. "Good-night, Steven."

"Good-night." The door closed firmly behind him.

———

When she awakened again, sunshine was flooding the bedroom, and the thin curtains at the window swayed gently, responding to a cooler breeze. The pervasive heat had vanished, perhaps washed away by the storm, and Leslie felt a surge of strength and well-being. Luxuriously, she rolled over and stretched like a cat. It was heaven! She hadn't slept this late since Penny . . .

Penny! She tumbled out of bed like a shot, grabbing her robe and racing for the bedroom door. Where was the baby? Aunt Mae had mentioned something about the room next door. She went barefoot down the hall she had barely noticed last night and stopped in front of the door next to her own. As she quietly opened the door, she saw another scantily furnished room, but dominating it was a large old-fashioned crib. Steven's crib, Leslie realized, and he had apparently brought it down from the attic last night while she slept.

Steven. The tearful middle-of-the-night scene trailed through her memory, leaving sorrow in its wake. Once again she had been foolish, revealing too much of herself to him, expecting a response he was incapable of giving. She knew now that he had taken her in out of a sense of exasperated pity, perhaps because he felt a bit responsible for her jobless state. And he no doubt would leave her alone from this point on. It was what he had promised, the only path they could follow.

Penny was not in the oversized crib, but the bags that held her supplies and the box of disposable diapers were lined against the wall, and Leslie wasn't worried. Somewhere in the recesses of this vast and wonderful house, the baby was being well tended. Leslie knew she could trust Aunt Mae.

Wandering back to her room, she perched on the window seat for a moment and gazed outside at the green panorama. The world looked newly washed and hung out to dry. Water still dripped from the eaves and tree branches, sun-sprayed leaves sparkling like diamonds as the fresh breeze stirred them. Leslie's eyes feasted on the distant corn crop ranging out toward the hills, then moved to a vegetable garden near the house's back door. It was a large plot, and, despite her city background, she knew enough to recognize the amount of labor required to produce those neat straight rows of green sprouts. The early pea crop was ready to harvest, tomato vines had blossomed, the strawberry patch was full, and feathery carrot tops were inches high.

The whole restful scene exalted her in a way she had never expected and filled her with energy. She had to get moving and get dressed, and explore the life that lay before her. Quickly she washed, pulled on jeans and a short-sleeved shirt, and impulsively braided her thick red-gold hair just as Dotty braided hers. Well, she was a farm girl now, wasn't she? Grinning at her reflection in the mirror, Leslie felt as if she had been reborn.

Downstairs, the large living area was empty. Leslie went on to the kitchen; once again it was a mess—dirty pans and sticky surfaces everywhere. Dotty, stirring a dubious-looking concoction at the stove, greeted her cheerfully. "You're just in time for lunch!"

"Lunch! Is it that late?" Leslie was dumbstruck.

"After eleven. But Aunt Mae said to let you sleep—you surely needed it."

"And I'm supposed to be taking care of *her*." Leslie felt like a fool. "Where *is* Aunt Mae?"

"Out under the big willow, with the baby. Ouch, that's hot!" Dotty dropped her spoon onto the floor with a clatter, leaving a greasy blob. Hastily Leslie left, unwilling to contemplate the lunch menu, and went through a back screened porch into a shady yard. Aunt Mae was sitting under the willow, and Penny lay beside her on a blanket, gazing in fascination at the rustling branches above her. It was a serene and restful portrait of two people at opposite ends of life enjoying each other very much. Leslie was touched.

"Aunt Mae, you are simply wonderful," she said, sinking down on Penny's blanket. "You've given me the best night's sleep I've had in weeks. But it's not a very good way for me to start my duties, is it?"

Aunt Mae looked at her. Her mouth was set in the already familiar firm line, but there was a hint of liveliness in the blue eyes. "It was on Steven's orders. He can be stubborn when he decides to be, and he insisted you needed plenty of rest."

"But who gave Penny all her feedings and took such good care of her?" Leslie stroked the baby's soft cheek, noticing her fragrant and rosy appearance.

"Steven and I, of course. He got up with her last night,

and I took over this morning."

A picture of Steven tenderly feeding the baby rose before Leslie's eyes. "I . . . I don't know what to say," she stammered, "except to thank you both very much."

"Well, you'll have to wait to thank Steven. He's back in the city."

"Already?" She felt a pang of disappointment.

"He had arranged for David Parker to give him a ride very early this morning. David's father is in the hospital there, recovering from a coronary bypass, and David's gone in to spend the day with him."

"Oh, I've met Mr. Parker." Leslie thought of the old man she had prayed with, the one who seemed to know Steven so well. "He's a sweet person and recovering very well."

Aunt Mae pounced on her words. "You're sure about that? It's true that Jed is going to be all right?"

"I'm positive. The surgery was a complete success."

"Well, that's a relief." Aunt Mae let out her breath. "Steven told me the same thing, but I thought he might just be trying to spare me some worry. You see, the Parkers are very special folk to us. They've always been our closest neighbors, and they've leased and farmed our land ever since Steven's parents died. David and Steven grew up together, and Steven is godfather to one of David's little sons. You'll like David's wife, Cindy. In fact, you'll like all the Parkers."

"If they're like Jed, I certainly will," Leslie nodded. "And he still lives with his son and works on the farm?"

"Oh yes," Aunt Mae sighed. "Just because Jed is getting a bit long in the tooth is no reason he can't be *useful,* you know." Her voice held a challenging note, but Leslie knew that Aunt Mae's aggravation was directed not at her, but at Steven.

"No reason at all," she agreed in a neutral tone.

"Not like *some* people, put out to pasture before they're ready just because of a little health problem." Aunt Mae was working into a full head of steam now, waiting for Leslie to argue with her. Leslie, however, had had too much experience with frightened patients to rise to the bait.

"You're absolutely right," she answered calmly. "Sometimes illness can be a temporary setback. But once someone has recovered, life can be as rewarding as it was before."

Aunt Mae faced Leslie squarely. "I can't recover from diabetes," she said, full of complaint. "It's going to be with me from now on, isn't it?"

"That's true," Leslie admitted. "But millions of people cope with it, including children, you know. They take care of themselves and follow their doctor's orders, and manage to live very happily."

Silence fell, and Leslie watched as Aunt Mae considered her words, a small gleam of hope lighting her eyes. Then it faded again. "Even if I were to handle the diabetes," she said slowly, "what good does it do if I have to leave the only home I've ever known?" She looked across the fields to the green hills, and Leslie took in what she saw—the mellow, beloved environment, more precious now because it was threatened.

"I can't tell you what to do about that problem, Aunt Mae," Leslie said quietly, "but I can help you to feel better. And maybe when that happens, you might have enough energy to make . . . other things happen, too."

Their eyes met in a moment of unspoken understanding. There really wasn't anything Leslie could do about Steven's future plans for Aunt Mae. But she did share the older woman's frustration, understood her fear, and for now, that seemed to be enough. "Well," Aunt Mae said grudgingly after a long moment, "I suppose—as long as you're here—you might as well teach me what you know about diabetes. And," as Leslie's face lit up in a smile, "can you do something about Dotty, too? She tries hard, but her cooking . . . well . . .''

"I'll do my best," Leslie promised, "in *every* way."

"I believe you will," Aunt Mae nodded. "You've had your share of trouble, haven't you? Widowed so young. And yet I can see it's only made you stronger. I respect that, child."

Leslie shifted uncomfortably. "I think I'll get started, Aunt Mae, right now."

After Penny had been put to bed and she and Aunt Mae had endured Dotty's lunch and waved the girl off, Leslie decided the first item on her agenda was to take a tour of the house and decide on a new routine, one with which they could all live comfortably. Dotty was out of her element in the kitchen, and Leslie would have to handle meal preparations to be sure Aunt Mae stayed on a proper diet. Despite her plumpness, Dotty looked strong and could probably tackle some much-neglected housework duties.

The house puzzled Leslie, not because of the layers of dust that lay on every surface, or the worn spots on the carpets and drapes, now mercilessly exposed in the brilliant sun. That was understandable since the house was too large to be adequately taken care of by one ill woman and a part-time helper. Nor was its shabbiness surprising; if the old dwelling was to be eventually sold, why spend money to replace furniture?

And yet, despite the beautifully tended vegetable garden which Aunt Mae cared for with obvious pride, there were no blooming pots inside the house, no pictures or ornaments, nothing to break the bleakness. Leslie couldn't help feeling that part of Aunt Mae's obvious depression stemmed from her drab surroundings. Perhaps when she had been teaching every day, the older woman hadn't had time to notice. But now that Aunt Mae had unwillingly retired to a life of growing vegetables—and little else—it seemed to Leslie that much could be done to brighten her home and, hopefully, her attitude, too.

Hesitantly, Leslie asked permission to investigate the attic and the old barn while Aunt Mae took her nap, and was granted it with a shrug, "Suit yourself." Aunt Mae exhibited little interest. "Don't see the point of fussing—the house and everything in it will be gone soon enough. But if you want to bother, go ahead."

Leslie accepted Aunt Mae's attitude for what it was, a refusal to get her hopes up, a morose settling for the inevitable. But she knew farms weren't that easy to sell. And if Aunt Mae's last days here could be brightened at all, it would be worth it.

Leslie began her tour with the second floor, peering into her own room, Penny's, and the two empty bedrooms at the end of the hall. Looking over their barrenness, she decided that Penny's room, at least, could be brightened with crisp new curtains and some colorful juvenile prints on the wall. Aunt Mae's room she would leave alone—the older woman was entitled to her privacy. And as for Steven's— she stood before the closed door with a qualm. His room was none of her business—*nothing* Steven did was any of her concern; but she paused for a moment, remembering again the caring way he had banished the terrors of her dream, his kindness in setting up the crib for Penny, then feeding the baby in the middle of the night. She wondered if he had gotten any sleep at all, with one thing after another, and whether he was, at the moment, enduring a grueling surgery schedule with more than the usual amount of fatigue.

Somehow, she knew he was not the sort of man to complain about the things he did for others, or even to regard them as especially noteworthy. They were simply an outgrowth of his Christian beliefs, and yet . . . she frowned. Steven had also reminded her that when people violate the rules, they get hurt. Had there been a note of grim satisfaction in his pronouncement? She had been a victim of his whiplash temper too, despite her attempts to explain. It was a strange blend of Christianity, she mused. Rigid black-and-white standards that had somehow led him to a career of serving others. Compassion for the masses, but little sympathy for one misguided girl.

Leslie flushed and bit her lip. Now *she* was judging *him*! And she would not compound the injury by opening his bedroom door and violating his privacy. Swiftly she turned to the last door, the attic stairway, and made her way to the top level of the house.

Almost two hours later Leslie emerged, dusty but triumphant. The attic was enormous, divided into five rooms and holding a veritable treasure chest. Small tables, a delicate mirror frame, even an antique rocker, most of the wood obviously stripped long ago by Steven's mother, and left to await final coats of varnish or wax. There were cedar chests, a church pew, rolls of wallpaper, faded but still lovely, and even some decorative flowerpots. Steven's mother had obviously loved her home very much, and had seen its possibilities with a clear eye. In whatever time remained, Leslie was going to do the very same thing.

The next few days only heightened Leslie's optimistic mood. The weather held, and the beauty of the slowly gathering summer seemed to call out to her. She took walks, traveling one special path that led to a tree stump in the hills, and sat surveying the pastures as if they were her own. But there would be more time for walks later.

Her most important order of business was to find the writeup on diabetes in one of the college textbooks she'd hung on to, and give it to Aunt Mae to read. She also showed Aunt Mae how to give herself her daily shot of insulin, by practicing first with a syringe and an orange. Leslie acknowledged Aunt Mae's fears as perfectly normal, drew up a sensible diet sheet, answered all the questions Aunt Mae asked—and by the end of the week, Steven's aunt had adopted an almost casual attitude about the whole matter, regarding the diabetes as nothing more than a bothersome nuisance.

There were other things to think about, too.

One of those was unlocking Dotty's grip on the kitchen. How could they go about it without offending her? She had noticed Dotty's fascination with the baby, and decided to use it as a bargaining chip.

"You know," she said casually a few days after her arrival on the farm, "I'm wondering, Dotty, if you might consider helping me out."

"Sure!" Dotty looked up from a mass of stringy dough. "You just ask, Mrs. Bennett."

Leslie smiled back. "First of all, you can call me Leslie. I'm not *that* much older than you!"

"Oh . . . well, sure." Dotty ducked her head in embarrassed pleasure.

"And second, Dotty, do you think we could rearrange the chores a bit? If I did the grocery shopping, since I can drive, and then took on most of the cooking, and you handled some morning housekeeping and Penny's breakfast and bath . . ."

"You mean it?" Dotty was awed. "I can take care of Penny?"

"If you wouldn't mind," Leslie answered. "Babies take up a lot of time, you know, and—"

"Mind!" Dotty looked ready to explode. "That's the best job of all, even better than cooking. You just make out a schedule, Mrs. Bennett—I mean Leslie—and we'll get it all done, you'll see!"

After a few days, Leslie and Aunt Mae were pleased to

observe that Dotty tackled her new routine with even more enthusiasm than the old one. The floors, windows, and furniture now showed evidence of polish and care. Even better, Dotty and Penny shared a precious hour every morning, and it was hard to decide who enjoyed it more. Listening to the baby's delighted coos as Dotty crooned to her, Leslie met Aunt Mae's eye in a conspiratorial wink. "Babies have a way of making things happen, don't they?" she grinned.

"Absolutely," Aunt Mae agreed, eating her perfectly poached egg with relish. "Or perhaps it's a determined young woman who won't take no for an answer!"

"Perhaps," Leslie grinned demurely, feeling almost giddy with unaccustomed triumph. Now if she could just figure out a way to get that cedar chest and one of the tables and maybe even that antique church pew down from the attic. The pieces needed only a final coat of stain and they would be ready to display and enjoy. But they were far too heavy for her to lift, even with Dotty's help. The farm definitely needed a man's hand, she realized, but there was no telling when Steven might return. And everything considered, Leslie decided, that was probably for the best, even if the furniture had to stay in the attic forever.

Unexpected help arrived, however, the very next morning. Leslie was out in the vegetable garden picking peas for a salad luncheon when she heard a rattly squeak and turned to see a red-haired boy about twelve pulling a wagon up the driveway. In the wagon, sitting in calm and solitary splendor, was a small gray goat. Leslie's fascinated gaze followed the pair until they stopped just inches in front of her. "Morning, ma'am," the red-haired boy said without preamble. "You the nurse?"

"Why . . . why, yes, I'm a nurse, but—"

"Name's Paul Ellis. I got Harry here, see. He's a goat."

"Yes, I can see that."

"Got a cut leg. I tried to fix it but it doesn't look too good."

Feeling as though she had just stepped into an episode of Alice in Wonderland, Leslie bent over the wagon and gingerly inspected Harry's foreleg. Harry gazed at her with mild eyes, seemingly oblivious to the angry gash running the length of his leg. "You've done a good job keeping it clean, Paul," Leslie pointed out. "But it won't heal right unless it's stitched. You need to take him to a veterinarian."

Paul squirmed and shuffled uneasily, too shy to meet her eyes. "Costs a lot of money," he mumbled.

"What?"

"Vets. Important for cattle and pigs. Not . . . not so important for pets."

"I see." Leslie interpreted his shorthand correctly. Hard-pressed farm families, like everyone else, had to spend their incomes on necessities first. It was unlikely that a scruffy goat would be high on most priority lists—except Paul's. He met her eyes now in mute appeal and there was nothing else to do but respond. "I've never sewed up a wound, Paul. I'm not a doctor or a vet, and I don't have the proper medication in my bag."

"Doesn't matter," Paul shrugged. "Dotty said you was a real nice lady—kind like Dr. Steve. That's why I came."

"Oh, you must be the Ellis boy who had the infected ear." She remembered the evening she'd arrived, when Steven had gone to examine an ill child. "Are you feeling better?"

"Yes, ma'am. Dr. Steve can fix anything, I guess. But he's not here. And Harry . . ." He glanced worriedly at his placid pet, and Leslie made up her mind.

"I've got some antiseptic that might dull the pain long enough for me to stitch the wound," she thought aloud. "But if it doesn't, Paul, I might hurt Harry. Are you willing to risk it?"

Paul's clear confident look gave her the answer. "We can do it," he said simply.

———————

About an hour later, Leslie realized in astonishment that they had. Despite her trembling fingers and pounding heart, she'd managed to treat Harry's cut, and the small goat was lying comfortably on a bed of hay in Aunt Mae's barn. "I think you ought to leave him here for the next few days, Paul, so I can watch for infection," she suggested.

"Okay. And thanks a lot. You were great."

"You were pretty good yourself. Not every boy could keep a goat calm."

"Oh, Harry's pretty easygoing." Paul dug in his jeans pocket. "Don't know how much you charge, ma'am, but I got a couple of dollars."

"Oh no," Leslie backed off. "There's no fee."

Paul stood his ground stubbornly. "An Ellis pays his debts," he announced, holding out the crumpled bills. "You got to take it."

"But . . ." Hastily Leslie prayed for inspiration, and it came. "I'm not a physician, Paul, so I can't accept money for my services. I think that would be illegal, you know, practicing medicine without a license."

"It would?" Paul hesitated.

"Something like that. But . . . would you consider barter?"

"Barter?"

She nodded. "I've got some furniture that has to be moved from the attic. Dotty and I can't lift it alone."

Paul was already striding masterfully out of the barn. "Just show me where you want it," he called over his shoulder, every inch the man in charge. "I'll handle it."

———————

It had been a full and interesting day, Leslie reflected that evening as she rocked Penny to sleep in her darkened bedroom. She had managed to treat a goat, something nursing school had forgotten to teach her, and the feeling of accomplishment was thrilling. She had added another young friend to a growing roster of people who seemed to like and accept her. How would they feel if they knew she was not the valiant widow she appeared to be?

Guiltily she shivered and held Penny even closer. No one would know, not as long as Steven stayed away from her. Without bearing the pain of his caustic comments, she could grow physically strong and emotionally secure—capable of mothering Penny in the best way. But if he visited the farm often, if his disturbing presence upset her hard-won peace of mind . . . well, she would worry about that when, and if, it happened.

Once again, as if in a dream, she felt his firm arms around her, the comfort of his murmured words as he protected her from her own fears. And then the image shattered, replaced by an angry Steven, and the reality of his contempt for her. *"People who violate the rules do get hurt,"* the image reminded her. *"You understand that, don't you?"*

"Yes," she sighed as she laid the sleeping baby in the crib. "I'm certainly beginning to understand that."

7

"We need packaged soups, crackers, cocoa mix, and flour." Standing on a chair, Leslie took inventory of the kitchen cabinets while Aunt Mae made a list. "The stew for supper is already on."

"Smells almost as good as the ones I used to make," Aunt Mae grudgingly conceded.

"But it may need more potatoes, and we're low on those, too. I think that's it." Leslie climbed down from the chair. "Unless you've thought of anything else that you need."

"Just that pink yarn for Penny's sweater. If you're sure you can find the dry goods shop."

Leslie hid a grin. Admittedly it was her first trip to town, but Aunt Mae had been hovering and clucking as if she were going off to Alaska. "Why don't you come with me?" Leslie asked impulsively. "You can keep me from getting lost, get the right yarn, and maybe see some old friends . . ." She was silenced by a baleful glance from the older woman, and realized that she had stepped across the invisible boundary. Aunt Mae was not interested in socializing—at least not yet—and she resented Leslie's prodding. And yet Leslie sensed that part of Aunt Mae's recovery depended on her taking an interest in something outside herself, perhaps feeling needed and useful again. But pushing the older woman before she was ready wasn't going to help. At least Aunt Mae was showing interest in a knitting project.

For the moment, it would have to do. "Sorry, Aunt Mae," Leslie smiled apologetically. "I didn't mean to boss you around. And besides, I appreciate you being right here— who else would feed Penny, keep an eye on Harry, and guard the stew from Dotty's tender touch?"

The blue eyes softened for a moment, but Aunt Mae was in a mood, and not easily won. "About that goat . . ." she began.

"He'll just be here for a few more days," Leslie assured her, grabbing her purse from the counter. "See you in a few hours." She dropped a kiss on Aunt Mae's brow, won a few more icy twinkles from her patient, and bounded down the stairs to her car.

Within moments she was on the thin ribbon of highway, winding her way toward town. The air was fragrant and bracing, the light so fresh it felt as if someone had torn the lid off the box she'd been living in. She was happy! It had been such a long time since she had sung aloud, so long since she had felt buoyant, confident, the sense that all was well. "Oh, Lord," she breathed, "thank you for this precious moment. And please let it last!"

It did, all the way to the small strip of stores which formed the nucleus of the village. She slid into a parking space outside a respectably sized supermarket, got out, and looked around. Down one street she could see a parade of small neatly kept houses, probably occupied by people who worked in the light industries on the other side of town. Down another street was a red brick building with a playground, now empty. Probably the school where Aunt Mae had taught. Buckets of brightly colored petunias sat cozily on the clean-swept walks, posters in store windows announced a local crafts fair to be held soon, and over the entire scene, the now-familiar hills kept their distant vigil. Leslie's serene attitude deepened.

Almost two hours later, she had crammed the Volkswagen to capacity with groceries, pink yarn, some mystery novels from the tiny branch library, and even a few larger-sized sleepers for Penny. It had been a wonderful experience. Everyone had been so welcoming and kind, and most of them seemed to know who she was, which explained the presence of two small tabby cats on the front seat, curled up in each other's embrace and snoring softly.

"You'd be amazed at the number of city people who abandon domestic pets in the country," Mr. Potts, the supermarket proprietor had confided to her indignantly. "They think the poor things can hunt and find food, but usually they die. Look, this one has obviously been wounded in a fight or something."

"It's really too bad about them," Leslie began. "They're awfully sweet, but—"

"I'd keep them, but the wife's allergic." Mr. Potts had steamrolled genially over her protests. "And you'd be better able to help them, being a nurse and all. Paul Ellis told us what a fine job you did with Harry. I'll just put them in your front seat, shall I?"

"Well . . ."

She looked now at the two newest members of a family that seemed to be increasing at an alarming rate, and started to laugh. She was no match for the soft twang of the hill people, the network of information they maintained with such artless grace, the gentle persuasion that prodded her into areas she never would have tried on her own.

"Hi, there. You're Leslie, aren't you?"

Surprised, Leslie turned to see a smiling blond woman just a little older than she. "Why, yes, I am."

"Mr. Potts told me you were still out front. I'm Cindy Parker." She stuck out a friendly hand. "Jed Parker is my father-in-law."

"Of course." Leslie clasped the hand warmly. "Aunt Mae spoke of your family. And Jed is very special, isn't he?"

"We can't wait until he comes home, can we, guys?" Cindy looked down and Leslie spotted two little towheaded boys peeking shyly from behind her jean-clad legs. "Say hi to Mrs. Bennett, boys. This is Matthew and this is Mark."

"No Luke and John?" Leslie grinned.

"Not yet, but we're hoping!" Cindy laughed, then turned serious. "Jed *is* all right, isn't he, Leslie? Steven says so, but we worry just the same."

"When I left the hospital he was coming along very well," Leslie assured her. "And you can trust Steven, you know. He's a wonderful physician."

"Don't we know it! Everyone here is still praying that he has a change of heart, even though it looks so hopeless."

"Is it really that impossible?"

"It appears to be. Everyone hoped Steven would be our doctor someday. We were all so proud of him when he went off to medical school. David and I had just gotten married, and I remember feeling so . . . so *excited* that one of our own, a simple hill boy, was going to do something so wonderful . . . and then everything changed—" She broke off, making a dive for Mark, who was attempting to reach the slumbering cats through Leslie's car window. "Want to go for coffee, Leslie? I promised these guys a treat."

"Sure. I guess the groceries won't spoil for a little while."

Sitting at a table outside the corner snack bar, Matthew and Mark dived into bowls of chocolate ice cream while Cindy warmed to her story. It concerned a man who had set off to school with the idea of helping his community, and come back more interested in acquiring position and power. "I'm not criticizing him," Cindy pointed out loyally, "because I believe there are many good ways to be a doctor, and a surgeon in a large city has a chance to heal a lot of people. But . . ." She trailed off uncertainly.

"But you don't think Steven's primary goal is to heal people?" Leslie asked gently.

Cindy shot her a grateful glance. "Not anymore, no. We hear he's become involved with some woman whose father is a bigwig on the hospital board. . . ."

"Rita Marchand. I've seen her."

"Really? Is she beautiful?"

"Very beautiful."

"Well . . . poor lamb. Perhaps he's dazzled by the kind of life she represents. In any case, he seems interested in staying on in Cincinnati now, instead of coming home and taking care of us." She hesitated, choosing her words with care. "I wouldn't be so upset about it if I thought he was happy, Leslie. But . . . somehow he's different now. I feel we're losing him completely."

"Perhaps he hasn't changed as much as you think," Leslie tried to comfort her. "I know he donates time to a street clinic. I met him there, actually." She thought of the stormy scene and blushed. Steven hadn't been a "poor lamb" then, by any means!

Cindy's eyes brightened. "Really? Then maybe his principles still mean something to him after all. Oh . . ." she shook her head vigorously. "How *can* I be so judgmental? I'm ashamed, Leslie. What you must think of us, especially considering everything that you've gone through yourself."

"Me?" Leslie asked, puzzled.

"Well, it can't be easy being a widow and left with a baby to care for." Cindy's eyes were sympathetic. "Dotty told us all about you—she thinks you're wonderful."

"Oh, Dotty exaggerates." Leslie flushed, uncomfortable at the undeserved praise. "I'm just an ordinary person, really."

"Well, Dotty needs a nice, normal role model," Cindy went on. "Her mother's been dead for a long time, you know, and that dad of hers . . . he means well but he's awfully backward and strict, too. A girl like Dotty needs some-one to talk to—oh!" She covered her mouth with her hand, eyes wide. "There I go again, gossiping! Leslie, I apologize. I'm hopeless!"

"Mommy hopeless!" Mark shouted gleefully.

"No you're not—" Leslie was laughing, too—"but I have to go, Cindy. Aunt Mae will think I've disappeared with the potatoes and yarn. It's been wonderful to meet you."

"Come over any time." Cindy's smile was traced with concern. "And if you get lonely . . . well, I've never experienced a loss like yours, but if you ever need a friend, I'm here."

"Thanks." Leslie's heart warmed despite her guilty pangs. "I'll remember."

Her spirits were still high as she rattled down Aunt Mae's bumpy driveway, parked as close to the porch as she could get, and gently disengaged one of the tabby cats from the front of her blouse. The other had gotten inside the bag of yarn goods and was noisily exploring the contents. Dotty had come down the stairs and was just approaching the Volkswagen when the cat stuck his head, entwined with pink yarn, out of the bag. Leslie started to giggle. "Dotty, look what the store had on sale!" She stopped. Dotty's eyes were red-rimmed, as though she had been crying, and she hoisted a bag of groceries out of the backseat without even glancing at the playful cat. Leslie watched, puzzled, as Dotty sidestepped Aunt Mae, who had just appeared on the porch, and disappeared inside. "What's the matter with Dotty?" she asked.

"Been sulking all day. Wouldn't talk to me." Aunt Mae's eyes were fastened on a gray tail waving out of the bag. "Do you want to tell me about *that*? Or should I guess?"

"Well, it's a cat, Aunt Mae."

"I can *see* that."

"And here's another. Mr. Potts was very persuasive. You see, they were both abandoned, and they need some tender loving care."

The older woman's hand was already caressing the smaller cat, even as she struggled to maintain her disapproving air. "Been a long time since we had any cats around," she mused softly. "But they'll have to stay outside, you understand."

"Oh, definitely." Keeping a straight face, Leslie reached for a grocery bag, her mission accomplished. She had no doubt that the cats would be sleeping on the foot of Aunt Mae's bed within a day or so. "Could you figure out what they should eat while I unload the car? And how is Penny?"

"Penny's fine." Dotty tramped past. "I'll be leaving now, Miss Leslie. I just stayed 'til you got home."

"Dotty, wait." Leslie put a gentle hand under the girl's chin and looked into her moist eyes. "You've been crying, haven't you? Can I help?"

"No." Dotty turned quickly away. "I . . . I can't talk about it."

"Well, if you change your mind . . ." Leslie called after her, but Dotty, pedaling her bicycle furiously, was already halfway down the driveway. "Poor kid," Leslie sighed. Sometimes teenagers didn't have to have major problems in order to be miserable. Sometimes it was hard enough just being sixteen. Leslie thought of Dotty's difficult and unsympathetic father, and decided she would definitely remember to pray for the girl and her father—and give Dotty some extra attention tomorrow.

Leslie followed Aunt Mae and the cats into the kitchen where the aroma of simmering stew welcomed her home. It seemed impossible that she and Penny had been in this warm, safe refuge for only a week. Her eyes fell on the baby, sitting on the kitchen table in her infant seat, fists waving, cheeks glowing, and a surge of gratitude rose within her for Aunt Mae who had made it all possible. "Aunt Mae, I . . ." she began, but the words, brimming from a heart that was almost too full, just wouldn't come. Instead she took the library books out of her shoulder bag. "I borrowed a few mysteries for us to read at night," she said.

Aunt Mae, busy mixing mash for the cats, looked at the titles and sniffed. "*The Case of the Abandoned Artist?* Goodness, child! I'd rather read the Bible."

"You would? Oh good, so would I." Leslie met Aunt Mae's surprised glance with delight. Another bond was beginning to form between them. "Then let's do that together, every night. And perhaps afterward, we can try a little of the *Abandoned Artist.* Just to see if we can figure out the puzzle, of course." She turned quickly, before Aunt Mae could object, and went out to the car to get another bag. When she returned, she noticed Aunt Mae's Bible sitting in readiness on the polished coffee table she'd brought down from the attic.

———

The peace lasted just a few more days until, late one afternoon, Leslie glanced out the front window and, with a sinking heart, watched a sleek dark car wind its way down the drive, with Steven at the wheel. Oh no, not now! Not when everything was going so well. Suddenly she was ashamed of her unreasonable panic, the selfishness that, unchecked, would prevent her from showing Steven the hospitality he deserved. It was his house, too. And he had driven a long, hot distance out of respect and love for his aunt. Calmer now, she went to the refrigerator and had a tall glass of lemonade poured as Steven climbed the front porch stairs and entered the hall.

"Hello," she said quietly. "It . . . it's nice to see you, Dr. Sawyer."

"Thank you, Leslie. It's nice to be here." He matched her formality, then looked at her steadily for a moment, taking in her long red-gold braid, the healthy flush on her cheeks. Silently she handed him the glass of lemonade and he drank deeply, still watching her over its rim. Then he looked around the house. Leslie watched his glance travel through the hallway, now furnished with a mellow highboy and buckets of greenery, to the living room where several pieces of restored furniture had been added. The room was brighter now since Leslie had stripped away the faded drapes to let in the sun. Frowning slightly, Steven walked past her to Aunt Mae's chair, where Penny's pink half-finished sweater lay in a tangle of yarn. "Aunt Mae is knitting a sweater?" he asked in disbelief. "She hasn't done any work like this since she got sick."

"She does when she has time for it," Leslie explained casually. "She's awfully busy, of course. There's the garden to weed, and her prize-winning corn bread to bake in case company drops in."

"Aunt Mae is making corn bread?"

"Which reminds me. You will stay for dinner, won't you, Dr. Sawyer?"

Without answering, Steven strode past her into the kitchen. She watched as his stunned gaze traveled past the scrubbed countertops to the baskets of geraniums hanging over the sink to the dutch oven on the stove's back burner where a simmering pot roast sent forth its mouth-watering aroma. Steven stood for a moment, trying to hide his astonishment, then cleared his throat. "I imagine I'll be able to stay. By the way, where is Aunt Mae?"

"Outside under the willow with Penny," Leslie told him. "They both have a little nap there almost every afternoon. Why don't you go and see her?"

"I will." When he had passed by, Leslie let out a sigh of relief and grabbed the cats, Ping and Pong, who had just ambled into the kitchen behind Steven. Somehow she knew it would be wiser if Steven remained ignorant about the cats. "Just for now, guys," she told them as she dashed madly upstairs and hid them in her own room. "He won't stay forever, and I'll bring you a treat later."

Hurrying down the stairs again, she began to set the dining room table with the blue woven mats and pretty white pottery she'd unearthed from an attic trunk. But the slam of the screen door interrupted. "Aunt Mae's still asleep," Steven announced from the dining room door. "And there's a goat in the barn."

Harry! She had forgotten him! Leslie's hands flew to her cheeks, and she stared guiltily at Steven. "Just a *little* goat . . ." she began.

His eyes met hers and suddenly the two of them stood locked as if they were touching each other. Was he angry? Or was that disturbing light in his eyes an expression of something else? Leslie didn't know, but her heart had started to pound, and she was sure that Steven could hear it from across the room.

The moment ended as abruptly as it had begun. "Steven, is that you?" Aunt Mae was calling from the yard, and he turned quickly and went back outside. It was only a brief reprieve, Leslie knew, only a short while before she would have to own up about Harry, and heaven only knew what else Steven would find to criticize. But she was grateful for the moment, grateful for the chance to quiet her inexplicably racing emotions. Quickly she finished setting the table, put Penny's bottle and a jar of strained cereal on to heat, and went to the backyard to scoop up the baby from her blanket in the shade.

"Dinner will be ready in a minute," she called to Aunt Mae, who was standing near the freshly weeded vegetable garden, apparently pointing out something of interest to Steven. Leslie tried to avoid his eyes, but couldn't help noticing that he seemed at a loss, as if nothing he was observing was at all what he had expected. *Good!* she thought wickedly. *Let him be confused for a change!*

Steven's bewilderment lasted all through dinner, first at the sight of the charming table, with flowers in the center, next at the mouth-watering pot roast and homemade hot apple pie. Leslie noticed he had two enormous helpings of everything. By the time the meal had ended and Aunt Mae reached for her Bible, he was thoroughly baffled. "We're on Proverbs, aren't we, dear?" she asked Leslie.

"Chapter three, I think." Leslie nodded and reached for her own Bible. She had mended the back lining, and the book now rested beside Aunt Mae's.

"And don't look so surprised, Steven," Aunt Mae said, flipping the pages. "After all, you were raised on the Bible."

"I'm not surprised," Steven protested, although it was obvious that he was.

Taking pity on him, Leslie attempted to explain. "We read the Bible every night after dinner, and sometimes in the mornings when Dotty is here."

"Although she likes *The Case of the Abandoned Artist* a little better, I suspect," Aunt Mae chuckled.

"I'm trying to persuade your aunt to teach a Bible study class for Dotty and some of the other young people in the area," Leslie went on. "She'd be wonderful."

"A class . . ." Steven began, but Aunt Mae was already reading.

"Trust in the Lord with all your heart
and lean not on your own understanding;
in all your ways acknowledge him,
and he will make your paths straight."

Trust in the Lord. . . . Leslie pushed away the anxiety rising within her. She was certainly failing on that score. Perhaps if she told Steven everything . . .

On an impulse she opened her mouth to ask if they could speak privately, but he had already risen and started for the door.

"Aunt Mae, if you'll excuse us, I'd like a word with Leslie," he announced over his shoulder. "We'll do the dishes when we get back."

"That's fine, dear." Aunt Mae beamed. "You did feed the cats, didn't you, Leslie?"

"Cats?" Steven stopped short.

"Uh . . . no, Aunt Mae." Leslie wanted to sink through the floor. "I . . . I put them upstairs and forgot about them."

"Never mind," Aunt Mae answered calmly. "We can do it when you return. And, Steven, you wouldn't mind looking at Ping, would you, just to make sure she's recovering?"

"Not at all, Aunt Mae," Steven replied smoothly, but his fingers gripped Leslie's arm in a firm grasp as he steered her to the door and down the steps. "Ping?" he demanded under his breath.

"And Pong," she admitted weakly. "They were strays. We . . . we've sort of nursed them back to health."

He let her go. "And the goat in the barn?"

"Oh, that's Harry. You don't have to worry about him—he'll be gone tomorrow. He belongs to Paul Ellis."

"Who stitched up his leg?"

"I did."

"*You* did?"

"He needed medical attention," she answered defensively, "and there wasn't anyone else. . . ."

"Yes," Steven sighed. "I know what vets cost. You don't have to explain. It was a very good job."

They had gone up the path to the tree stump and sat upon it now, almost companionably. Before them the sun was setting, the western sky reflecting its glory in shining pastels, rosy pink and pale blue, puffy clouds edged with gold. The light was so clear Leslie could see the outline of each hill, each leaf on the nearby bushes and trees. It was hers, only for the moment perhaps, but while it lasted, hers. *Oh, God, thank you for all of it.*

She knew it was the moment to confess, to tell Steven of the masquerade she had been guilty of perpetrating, to ask for his forgiveness and perhaps even his understanding. "Steven," she began, but as he turned to her, she saw his formidable expression and her heart sank, for she knew he was, once again, angry with her.

"In all fairness," he said as if she had not even spoken, "I have to give you credit. Aunt Mae looks wonderful, and she seems settled about the whole diabetes business. I haven't checked her yet, but I'd guess she's in finer physical condition now than she's been in many months. Even better, she's getting interested in her surroundings again. The house looks nice—I noticed some of Mom's things around—"

"I hope you don't mind," Leslie interjected hastily.

"No, not really."

"Then why—?"

"Why am I aggravated? Because you're making this house, this *life*, too attractive to Aunt Mae, Leslie."

"I don't understand," Leslie protested. "I thought you wanted your aunt to be well and happy."

"Of course I do. But I don't want her directing her energy and interest to the farm. I'm trying to persuade her to move to the city, and then you come along and—"

"And give her what she's needed all along, some faith in the future!"

They were standing, facing each other now, adversaries squared off for the familiar combat. "That's not fair, but I'm not going to argue about it," Steven retorted. "Instead I'm going to remind you that, as your employer, I have certain rights. One of them is to insist you stop turning my property into a . . . a home for wayward strays. And while we're at it, you can stop thinking about starting Bible classes, with people tramping all over the place. . . ."

"Aunt Mae would love it!"

"I'll be the judge of that! You just do your job—"

"This *is* my job!"

"Or you and Penny will have to leave!"

She stopped as if she had been slapped, utterly shocked at the threat, and saw that Steven was as shaken as she. "You wouldn't . . . you promised . . ." she whispered through wooden lips.

"Leslie, wait . . ." he reached for her but she whirled and started to run. He was right behind her and she felt his hand on her arm, pulling her back to him. "Leslie, please wait . . ." Steven swung her around to face him again. She saw the startled look on his face and the impulse to kiss him was automatic and instinctive, leaping from some hidden inner source she couldn't explain. But she couldn't act on it, or she would have far more to lose than a place to live. Blindly, she eluded his grasp and ran back to the house, back to the secrets she now had to keep, whatever the price.

8

*M*orning came with gray clouds covering the landscape, breaking the chain of perfect days with rain that rattled against the windows and drenched the somber hills. It suited Leslie's mood to perfection. Awakened several times by the familiar and terrifying nightmare, she sat now in the deep window seat with Penny nestled in her lap, staring at the rain in exhaustion. In a moment she would dress and bring the baby downstairs for her breakfast. She would have to start the day as if nothing had happened, even though Steven's car still stood in the clearing, and Steven himself was obviously sleeping in the room down the hall instead of back in Cincinnati where he belonged.

She hadn't seen him after her wild dash across the fields. Pleading a headache, she had burst in upon a startled Aunt Mae, took Penny, and gone up to bed early. If Steven had followed her—which she doubted—she had eluded him, at least until now.

Steven. How he confused her. She had every right to hate him; but as a Christian, she couldn't. And yet, were her feelings really so negative? Every word he said, every arrogant glance from those light eyes irritated her. Yet those rare times when he smiled . . . she found herself remembering every one of them, and her cheeks burned.

Was she attracted to Steven? Had she really wanted to kiss him last night? Or was her yearning to be enfolded in a pair of strong arms just a reaction to the fear and loneliness of the last few desperate months? That had to be the explanation, she told herself briskly. She was not a silly schoolgirl, ready to be bowled over by the first attractive man to come along. But she certainly wasn't acting maturely, letting her temper run away with her whenever Steven glared in her direction. She realized, sadly, that she wasn't letting God shine through her with His gifts of gentleness and self-control.

And why would she be attracted to someone cruel enough to control her with threats? If only she could fling the job in his face, stalk off, and never look back. . . . Penny cooed, and Leslie cooed back. "No, my little love," she reminded the baby as well as herself, "you and I won't be grandly announcing our resignations, no matter how much satisfaction it would give us. Steven has us right where he wants us, at his mercy."

When she brought Penny downstairs a few minutes later, however, she discovered an unexpectedly pleasant scene, the opposite from last night's quarrel. Coffee was perking, some of Aunt Mae's corn biscuits were warming in the oven, and Steven was whistling tunelessly as he dried a few leftover dishes. He met Leslie's surprised look with studied casualness. "I thought I heard you stirring. Have some coffee."

"I . . . thanks, but I have to feed the baby first. Why are you up so early?"

"Doctors always get up early."

"Yes, I suppose they do." Unnerved under his scrutiny, Leslie shifted Penny to her hip as she fumbled for the small chair. Steven grabbed it and took the baby from her before she had time to protest. "Here, let me feed her." He hoisted Penny effortlessly into the chair. "I want to see how she's getting along, anyway."

"So you can report me to the authorities if you find anything wrong?" The sarcastic jibe was out of her mouth before she could stop it, and she flushed. "I'm sorry. That was a terrible thing to say."

"You and I seem to say a lot of terrible things to each other," Steven replied calmly. "I'm sorry, too, for allowing things to get out of hand last night."

"Well then . . ." An awkward silence fell. Was he taking back his threat? Steven said no more, and so Leslie poured a cup of coffee and took it up to Aunt Mae, then returned and poured two more. "Cream or sugar?" she asked Steven, amused to note that his shirt was spattered with the cereal Penny was spitting at him.

"Just black." He wiped Penny's mouth and grinned at the baby. "She's in great shape, Leslie, alert and healthy. When do her casts come off?"

"The end of July." Surprised at his pleasant tone, Leslie matched it. "We have a late-afternoon appointment at St. Luke's."

"I see." Steven gave her another steady gaze. "The country air must be good for you, too. It's obvious that you're quite a bit healthier than you were just a few weeks ago."

Leslie took a deep breath. "Which is why the baby and I need to stay here a while longer, Steven," she said quietly. "So even though I don't agree with your wishes concerning Aunt Mae, I want you to know that I'll . . . I'll carry them out."

"I have left you no other choice, is that it?" Steven's tone was suddenly cool.

"Well . . . I guess it's just that I want to be honest with you."

"You, honest?" He laughed without mirth and her heart sank.

"What do you mean?" she demanded.

"I mean that all your high-sounding statements about honesty, and reading the Bible with Aunt Mae, and all these works of mercy for the neighbors . . . it's all rather pointless, isn't it?"

She saw where he was leading, and she tensed. "Pointless? Yes, I suppose to someone like you, it would be."

It was his turn to be defensive. "Someone like me?"

"Yes. Someone who regards Christianity as just a bunch of rules or words, something that's conveniently trotted out on Sundays. Have you ever heard of repentance, Steven?"

"You're trying to tell me you've repented?"

She turned away from his angry challenge. "I'm not trying to tell you anything," she said tiredly, "except that I will honor your rules about Aunt Mae."

"My *rules* . . ." Steven repeated grimly. "I see. Then you give me your word? No more animals, no Bible classes, no excitement . . . just normal nursing care."

"As you've pointed out, you've left me no other choice."

The shrill ring of the telephone broke their angry confrontation, and Steven snatched it up. "Yes, Ed, I got in last night. Hold it, now, calm down . . . can she talk? Does anything look broken? No, the ambulance might not get there for hours. Don't move her, Ed. I'll be there as soon as I can." Hanging up, he looked past Leslie to where Aunt Mae stood in her bathrobe. "Remember Ellen Carney? She and her husband were in my class. Her car went off the road just now, probably hit by a coal truck."

Aunt Mae shook her head. "You'll have to go, dear. Can I help?"

Steven was already at the door but he turned and looked at Leslie. "You could lend me your nurse."

"I'll come." Their quarrel forgotten, Leslie didn't even wait for Aunt Mae's permission, but followed at Steven's heels.

Steven carried a virtual pharmacy in his medical bags,

he assured Leslie as they drove under gray scudding clouds. He had everything from anesthesia to rudimentary operating tools to antibiotics and plaster for casts; rural physicians knew that the emergencies they faced were as varied as their patients, and they had to be prepared for anything. "There are a lot of car accidents up in the hills," he explained. "The hairpin turns are tricky and some folks drive faster than they should. Then add those to the other medical emergencies that arise. . . . I've set fractures, delivered babies, treated all kinds of gunshot wounds—it's an exciting way to practice medicine because you never know what you'll be doing next."

Leslie clung to the edge of her seat as Steven took the winding turns too quickly for her own comfort. She sensed that in the midst of his concern for his classmate, there was also an element of excitement. The wind blew his dark hair across his forehead, making him look almost boyish, animated, caught up in the challenge of the emergency. She was in tune with his thoughts, too: How badly was Ellen hurt? Could they provide the skill and help she needed? By the time they reached the roadside scene, Leslie was as emotionally involved as he.

Fortunately, Ellen had skidded into a gravel clearing rather than going over the edge of the bluff when the truck hit her, but the impact had broken the window on the driver's side, and glass lay everywhere. A scrunched door prevented Ellen from getting out of the car, and she was half lying, half sitting behind the steering wheel. As they pulled up, Ed Carney, a tall, lanky young man, left his post beside the car and reached Steven in two or three strides. "I heard the crash from the house, Dr. Steve. It was fierce. And there's so much blood. Thank God you're here." The two men embraced with no trace of embarrassment, and Leslie was touchingly aware of the deep and long-standing affection they shared—how much, in fact, everyone seemed to love Steven. Was it only she who caught the brunt of his temper, the darker side of his nature? There was no time to think about that, for Steven was already at the car, bending in to talk quietly with Ellen. She was crying, Leslie noted as she dragged the medical bags out of the trunk, but she did not seem hysterical. Although there was quite a bit of blood and a probable concussion, judging from the angry gash in Ellen's temple, Leslie doubted that they were dealing with a spinal injury or punctured lung. As she reached Steven, she could see her own impressions confirmed by his silent nod. Ellen had been lucky.

The next hour flew by as the men wrenched the car door open, carefully removing the young woman, and Steven examined her carefully as she lay on the damp grass. These were the episodes that separated the capable physicians from the truly superb, Leslie realized, because Steven had no machines, lab tests, or other aids to help him in his diagnosis. Instead, he had to rely strictly on his hands and eyes, and that nebulous quality called instinct. Yet Leslie was certain that he had missed nothing.

As Ed hovered nearby, joined by two young girls who were the image of their mother, Steven stitched, and Leslie cleansed each wound first with bottled water and antiseptic. Steven was as precise as if he were performing surgery, and although Leslie had never worked in an emergency room, she found herself once again anticipating his needs—choosing a small-sized scissors, grabbing extra cotton—before he needed to ask. Steven set two broken fingers, closed the angry gash on Ellen's forehead, and finally sat back on his heels with a small sound of satisfaction. "You've lost too much blood, Ellen," he told her, "but if you promise to behave yourself and lie on the couch and eat plenty of good food, I think you can skip a transfusion."

Sleepily, Ellen flashed a dimple through her tear-streaked face. "Still the same old bossy Steven," she murmured. "You haven't changed a bit."

"Neither have you," Steven countered, straight-faced. "You always were a terrible driver."

Ed Carney started to laugh, and so did the children, soon joined by Leslie, who was relieved now that the pressure had passed. She met Steven's amused gaze again, and the look they shared was one of mingled triumph and perfect unity. They had done it. Ellen hadn't bled to death alone on the shoulder of a highway. She would have many fruitful years ahead of her—because of them.

"It was just—unbelievable." Leslie was still talking about it an hour later as they bounced down the rutted tracks toward home. The Carney family had touched her with their gratitude, their dignity in the midst of a poor but polished cabin, and absurdly, Leslie felt like bursting into tears. To cover her feelings she was chattering instead, reliving each moment of the emergency. Steven seemed to know how she felt, silently sharing her reaction, until finally she wound down. "I . . . I just don't understand how you can give up all this . . . this challenge for a job in Cincinnati."

Belatedly she regretted her words, for Steven's fingers tightened on the steering wheel. Instead of lashing out at her, he answered quietly. "You know, Leslie, there are sick people in Cincinnati, too."

"I know. I'm sorry, Steven. I have no right to tell you what to do."

"No, you don't. But you might be interested to know that a member of the board at St. Luke's is spearheading a drive for a brand new street clinic, a good facility where a lot of poor people could be helped."

"That would be wonderful."

"It would be for me, too. Whoever is appointed clinic administrator has to agree to certain conditions, but I know this board member very well, and he's hinted that if I were willing, I could be appointed to the job. I could do a lot of good there."

"Oh. Certain conditions?"

"Yes." Steven did not elaborate, and Leslie stared out the window as silence fell, willing her suddenly pounding heart to stop. She knew perfectly well what Steven was talking about. The board member, no doubt, was Rita Marchand's wealthy father, and the "condition" was probably the marriage of Rita and Steven! Anger rose swiftly within her, anger and another feeling she couldn't identify. He was allowing himself to be *purchased*, selling his personal life and his medical talent, too, for the power, money, and prestige of an executive. Anyone could run a hospital! Well, perhaps not . . . but how many men had the touch of healing in their hands, the concern for the sick, the dedication to keep learning, keep trying? She felt literally sick at the thought of him throwing it all away.

Her feelings, all of them, seemed to be erupting in a huge tidal wave of emotion, but she swallowed hard against it. She would not cry in front of Steven, or leave herself open for any of his stinging barbs. Nor would she intrude into his life with unwanted advice. She clasped her hands tightly together, then heard Steven clear his throat and shift positions behind the wheel. "I sensed that you were praying today as we worked on Ellen," he said slowly. "Do you often do that?"

"Well, yes," she answered, taken aback. "I know that a lot of things can block the healing process—unresolved anger, for example, or unforgiveness—so I pray that the patient lets go of these emotions, and that the physician does, too. That way healing can flow more fully, you see."

"I never thought about praying like that," Steven mused. "I guess I'm more formal. You know, rules and regulations and those things."

He was teasing, and Leslie blushed. "I shouldn't have

attacked your faith. And there's nothing wrong with rules—God gave us His own standard of behavior in the Ten Commandments, and if everyone followed *those* rules, we'd have heaven right here on earth. But . . ."

"But?" Steven encouraged.

"Well, there's more," she continued reluctantly. He would mock her again. Yet she felt compelled to speak. "Christianity is more than rules for the intellect; it's an attitude that springs from the heart. Jesus told us to love and forgive one another, even if we don't *feel* loving and forgiving. We have to act that way, and then sooner or later we become that way." She wasn't making any sense, but Steven was listening intently.

"And," he asked finally, "that's why you pray for me?"

"Yes," she admitted. "I . . . I don't think you forgive very easily. I do pray about that because a hardened heart could affect your work."

She waited uncomfortably for the derisive reply but none came. By the time she had drawn together enough courage to look at Steven, he was heading down Aunt Mae's driveway. Pulling to a stop in the clearing, he made no move to turn the ignition off. "I'm going back to Cincinnati now," he told Leslie, staring ahead through the windshield. It had started to rain again. "Tell Aunt Mae I'll see her soon. And try to get up to take a look at Ellen Carney this week. Make sure the stitches aren't becoming infected—you know what to look for."

"You're going *now*? Why so soon?"

"I believe we have an agreement, you and I," Steven pointed out quietly. "I'm supposed to refrain from harassing you, isn't that it?"

"Well, yes, but . . ." She felt awkward and ashamed. "You haven't really done that. At least not today."

Steven laughed shortly. "Well, the day is still young, and I find I'd rather spend it safely in Cincinnati where things will no doubt be calmer. As long as you don't forget our other agreement while I'm gone."

"The other one?"

"The one where you promised to limit yourself to taking care of my aunt—and that's *all*."

Leslie's mouth dropped. After the exhilarating morning they had just shared, the bond of trust that she, at least, had thought was growing between them, they were now back to the very beginning. Steven couldn't wait to leave her irritating presence and get back to the city, where a real woman, glamorous and devoted, awaited him. And now that Leslie had confessed that she prayed for him (when she wasn't arguing with him) ... well, Steven was too self-sufficient, too proud to regard that as a kind gesture. He had obviously taken it as an insult, and was striking back at Leslie, reminding her of her position as puppet on his string. His unspoken threat hung between them: "Do it my way. Or pack your things."

Leslie's shoulders sagged in defeat. "You drive a hard bargain, Steven," she whispered, blindly reaching for the door handle. "But then, I should be getting used to it by now, shouldn't I?"

"What is that supposed to mean?" Steven demanded, but she had stepped from the car and was climbing the porch steps. The tires squealed in protest as his car turned and sped down the bumpy drive.

The house was quiet, cool, wrapping her in a welcome aura of acceptance after Steven's latest rejection. But it felt curiously empty, too, as if something vital that ought to be there was missing. Was it Steven's presence? Would she *never* still the trembling yearning that rose within her at such peculiar times? Oh, it amused him to manipulate her, but to a small degree, he needed the temporary help she could give Aunt Mae. Leslie fell far short of his lofty standards— her presumably soiled past guaranteed it. And Steven's future lay in another direction entirely. A vision of Rita Marchand, sophisticated and rich, started to arise, but by sheer willpower, Leslie banished both Steven and Rita from her mind.

Penny was fussing halfheartedly, almost as if she were talking herself into it, and Leslie followed the sound into the kitchen where the baby sat in her little chair. Dotty was nowhere to be seen, which seemed unusual, until Leslie heard a muffled sob from the back porch.

The poor kid. Leslie couldn't solve her own problems, but maybe she could solve someone else's. What teenager didn't need a friend now and then?

"Dotty?" Gently she approached the girl as she sat huddled on the porch swing. "Can I help, honey?"

"Oh . . ." Dotty lifted a streaked face, and Leslie melted at the misery she saw there. "I'm in so much trouble, Leslie. I don't know what to do."

"Can you talk about it?" She sat down and slipped an arm around Dotty's quivering shoulders. Dotty sank against her as a fresh wave of sobs overtook her.

"Can . . . can you lend me some money, Leslie?" she pleaded finally. "It's awfully important."

"Some money?" Leslie thought for a moment. Her checkbook balance had improved over the past few weeks, but she was saving it for Penny's orthopedic bill. "Sure I can. How much do you need?"

Dotty raised her face. "Enough to pay for an abortion."

"Oh, Dotty!" Leslie was stunned. "Oh, honey, no!"

"Oh yes!" Dotty started to cry again. "And . . . I suppose you'll think I'm a terrible person now and . . . and hate me."

"You're not a terrible person, and I could never hate you, Dotty. I guess I was surprised." She tightened her grip on the trembling girl. "I didn't know you were . . . involved with anyone."

"I'm not. I mean . . . he's just a boy from town. We don't want to get married. But I know my dad will want me to when he finds out."

"Your father doesn't know?"

"No—and he can't. He'd be so angry with me, Leslie. I've sinned against God and humiliated my dad—that's what he'd tell me." Another wave of weeping overtook her.

"Dotty, you have done something wrong, that's true." Leslie tried to keep calm. "But an abortion would only make things much worse. Just because abortion is legal doesn't make it moral. You're a Christian, honey. You know that."

Dotty kept crying. "I know it, but I'm such a failure. How could God ever forgive me? I've thought about everything a million times these last few weeks. But I feel like I'm in a box now, and an abortion's the only way out. Please help me."

"Dotty, God's love for you hasn't changed because of what you've done. He only wants you to reach out to Him for help now." Leslie held the sobbing girl while voices from years past began to surface in her mind, all with the same plea. "I'm pregnant. Help me!" How many girls had she soothed and talked to on the telephone hotline she and the other volunteer college students worked on at the local pro-life ministries? She remembered the many times she had calmed an incoherent caller and directed her to an agency or a family who would willingly board her and love her through her pregnancy. How many bags of used baby clothes and baby food had she collected through the years? How many families had she helped to reconcile? How many women had she visited in the maternity wards, grateful beyond words that someone had provided them with an alternative to the abortion clinic, with the chance to choose life?

And how many callers had let despair and fear overwhelm their sense of right and wrong, and had chosen what surely seemed the easier route? She thought of the many aborted babies, the anguish of their mothers, an anguish that might follow them all their lives—and the familiar sense of helplessness overcame her. *Lord, it's all too much. They're killing your creation, and I try to stop it, but I haven't got the power, I haven't the wisdom or the words. . . . Please help me.*

The unmistakable answer came once more, gently penetrating the layers of fear. It wasn't necessary to have the power or all the answers, she knew, as she had always known. She only needed to be a channel of His love for this young girl right now.

Dotty had quieted now, leaning in exhaustion against her, and hope flooded Leslie's spirit. "We're going to work this out, Dotty," she said firmly. "I promise you that. You're not alone anymore."

9

"*I* just can't believe it, Leslie, that something so tiny could be so perfectly formed already." Dotty stared at the book's photos in awe.

"Some*one*," Leslie corrected, smiling. "Don't forget—your baby had a heartbeat and a brain wave and even little hands and feet before you were sure he or she existed."

Dotty was reading one of Leslie's old nursing texts in fascination. Leslie was glad she had phoned a former roommate in Minneapolis and asked her to send the books on. Yet she was preoccupied—and even a little frightened—by her friend's unexpected comment: "Sure, I'll mail the books, Leslie. And by the way, did that guy ever catch up to you?"

"What guy?" Leslie had asked.

"Some former boyfriend, he said. He snooped around here for a while, but no one knew where you had gone. To tell you the truth, he really didn't seem your type. Kind of rough."

"Oh . . ." *Could it have been Tony?* Leslie didn't want to believe that he would go to such lengths to hunt her down, but surely her trail would have ended in Minneapolis, especially since no one there even knew about Penny. She would have to leave the matter in God's hands, no matter how nervous she was beginning to feel, and concentrate on Dotty instead.

A week had passed since the teenager's sobbing con-

121

fession, and she seemed more subdued now that someone shared her burdens. Leslie was helping her learn something about fetal development. It had been her experience that most young girls were tricked into believing that abortion was an easy solution, the unborn child dismissed as "a blob." Leslie had met many women who were shocked to discover how *human* their child was, even at eight or ten weeks' gestation. Many of them, fortified with the facts, had become more concerned about protecting their child than destroying it.

"It's a real baby, just like Penny," Dotty mused now.

"Just like all of us, only smaller," Leslie pointed out. "Remember when God said to Jeremiah—'Before I formed you in the womb, I knew you'? He was telling all of us that life begins at conception. And the Bible tells us over and over again to choose life instead of death."

On a more practical level, Dotty also deserved to know that plenty of later health problems could result if she underwent an abortion, things they probably wouldn't warn her about at an abortion clinic. Infections, damage to the womb, a higher chance of future miscarriages. Leslie had even heard one physician say that in his view, a teenager having an abortion would suffer emotional trauma for the rest of her life. This was not a future that Leslie would wish on Dotty or any other girl. They deserved guidance and the *right* kind of help.

The biggest part of the problem was that Dotty felt so alone. It was no wonder that she was tempted to end her baby's life, for how could she get through a pregnancy by herself? "My dad would throw me out for sure, Leslie," Dotty had confided. "And I don't want to get married even if the baby's father did—which he doesn't. I was hoping to go to college, to make something of myself. I even applied for a student loan, but now, if I have the baby, I won't finish high school on time. . . ."

"Dotty, why did you get so involved with any boy?" Leslie asked in exasperation, even though she sensed the answer.

Dotty's eyes filled with tears. "I didn't really want to. I had an awful feeling about it. But . . . life gets so lonely sometimes. And when someone says he loves you, and you really need to be loved . . ."

Her voice died away, and Leslie nodded in understanding. She had heard the same story so many times before. Teenagers who had a strong sense of their own worth, a self-respect developed through years of living in a disciplined and loving home, seemed to avoid premarital pregnancies. Some, of course, might be swept off their feet in a momentary passion, others might succumb to peer pressure and the "everybody's doing it" attitude, but most avoided temptation because they knew where it could lead.

It seemed that girls who had been deprived of parental love, especially those with harsh, disinterested, or absent fathers, were the vulnerable ones, so eager for affection and approval that they were even willing to go against their consciences to get it. Dotty fit the pattern to a T.

Now, however, the teenager lifted her eyes from the book and stared at Leslie with new awareness. "I don't know what to do," she admitted. "The baby is a real person already. How can I destroy it? But what other choice do I have?"

Leslie took a deep breath. "Suppose you didn't have to worry about where to live or how to support yourself for the next few months until the baby was born. Would you have it then?"

Dotty thought, chin in hand, eyes closed. "How could I raise it, all alone?"

"No one is asking you to make those decisions, Dotty, at least not now. God gives us just one day at a time, you know. There are millions of childless couples who would give anything to adopt your baby. And there are many single mothers who keep their babies and raise them."

"Yes, ma'am, I know. Like you."

"Well, yes. You made one mistake, Dotty. But you and God can turn that mistake into something beautiful—if you want to."

"Oh, I do, Leslie. But how?"

Leslie bit her lip. "I don't know, honey. Not yet, anyway. But I'll find out."

———

She couldn't ask Steven. Hadn't she just promised him to nurse Aunt Mae in an atmosphere of peace and quiet and dullness? To stop, as he put it, doing works of mercy for the neighbors? To go against his wishes was to risk her own security as well as Penny's. But this was quite literally a matter of life and death. The natural panic that Dotty was experiencing could push her into making a damaging decision. And Leslie knew only too well how a wrong choice could affect one's whole future—she was a perfect example of that. While she couldn't undo her own mess, perhaps she could prevent another one from taking hold. Aunt Mae would have to know.

She found Aunt Mae in the living room examining the last few pages of *The Case of the Boring Bookworm*, their current mystery. "Aunt Mae, you're peeking!" Leslie accused, trying not to laugh.

"I am not. I'm simply picking the book up from the floor."

"I'll bet! Just because Dotty solved *The Case of the Abandoned Artist* before you did . . ."

"That has nothing to do with it." They grinned comfortably at each other, and then Leslie pulled up a stool. "Speaking of Dotty," she began.

An hour later they were still deep in discussion. Aunt

Mae, after her initial distress, felt strongly that Dotty should move in with them until the baby was born, providing her father consented. "I can certainly keep her up-to-date on her schoolwork so she can graduate on time," Aunt Mae pointed out. "She might place the baby for adoption and go on to college, but that's up to her."

"I agree that we must provide more for Dotty than platitudes," Leslie nodded. "If Christians are going to speak out against abortion—or anything else—we must be willing to help those who are victimized by it. But . . ." Mindful of Steven's command and her promise to him, she tried to tread gently. "I was thinking more of finding Dotty a home for unwed mothers or maybe a family that would take her in."

"There's no such home around here or I would have heard of it," Aunt Mae said. "And we're a family, aren't we? What's wrong with you, girl? Of all people, I thought you'd be the first one to open the door to Dotty."

"Oh, Aunt Mae . . ." A vision of Steven pitching her and Penny out of that same door rose before her. It was followed by a vision of Dotty, trudging hopelessly into an abortion clinic because no one had cared enough to help.

There was, of course, no question that they'd help her. "I'll see if there's an extra bed in the attic." Leslie walked over to Aunt Mae and gave her a hug. While she did not normally welcome displays of affection, when Leslie released her this time, she looked pink and rather pleased.

———

The days passed in an uneasy sort of peace. Dotty talked to her father about her situation and he was as angry as she had predicted. Sometime during the next month, she would move her things into Aunt Mae's house; it seemed the best arrangement for everyone.

Leslie maneuvered the pickup truck back through the

hills and was relieved to find a dimpled Ellen Carney "on the mend."

On Friday, as she was doing the weekly grocery shopping, she ran into Cindy Parker. The slim young woman greeted her with a hug. "Hi, Leslie. How's Ellen Carney doing?"

"Honestly," Leslie laughed, "the news network around here is unbelievable. What do you use—jungle drums?" Cindy laughed. "But you needn't worry—Ellen's recovering very well. How's your father-in-law?"

"David brought him home from the hospital, and he's been champing at the bit. Wants to get up on the tractor and back to work." Cindy grinned. "David and I thought we'd ask some people over for a barbeque after the craft fair on Sunday to give him some diversion. You'll come, won't you?"

"Oh, I'd forgotten about the fair." Leslie looked now at the colorful poster. "I wonder if I can get Aunt Mae to go."

"She used to love it; in fact, she used to exhibit the things she had knitted," Cindy explained. "Maybe she'll come if she knows you're all invited to our house. I suspect she'd like to see Jed—they've always been kind of sweet on each other."

"Really?" Leslie was fascinated. "Aunt Mae and Jed? What a great combination!"

Cindy clapped her hand over her mouth. "There I go again, gossiping. Forget I said anything, will you, Leslie?"

"Consider it forgotten," Leslie promised, and proceeded to think about it all the way home.

Aunt Mae did initially balk at the idea of the fair, insisting that Leslie go alone. But, as Cindy had predicted, when she heard about the dinner invitation she relented slightly. "I suppose you might pick me up after the fair," she told Leslie. "I might put in an appearance at the Parkers' for an hour or so." Casually she eyed the contents of her closet.

"Sorry you can't make it to the fair," Leslie countered breezily. "I'd planned to take Penny and spend the day. I've never been to a mountain craft fair, and I especially wanted to see the knitting displays."

"Well, they're not what they used to be," Aunt Mae huffed, but she was already holding a patchwork skirt up to herself in the mirror. Leslie made a hasty retreat. Jed Parker must be a powerful draw; Aunt Mae was actually leaving the farm for the first time in ages.

————

Sunday dawned bright and beautiful and Aunt Mae had changed her mind about the fair. After attending church, feeding Aunt Mae and Penny, coaxing her hair into a ponytail, packing the car with a day's supply of blankets, snacks, and diapers, then reassuring Aunt Mae that Ping and Pong would be perfectly safe in her absence—and that she looked absolutely beautiful and no one would ever guess that she had been sick—Leslie was having second thoughts about the whole venture. However, once they were actually on the road, her spirit lifted. It would be a good day, she was sure of it. Especially since Steven was obviously in Cincinnati and knew nothing—yet—about Dotty and her plans to move in. Leslie might as well enjoy whatever reprieve she had.

They reached the fairgrounds where people were already mingling, ambling from tent to tent, chatting easily with old friends. Small children dashed excitedly from the little merry-go-round to the concession stand where cotton candy was a big seller. It was obviously one of the major social events in the area, and Leslie found herself warming once again to these proud, yet gentle, people and the customs that bound them together.

She got Penny settled in the stroller, then helped Aunt Mae out of the Volkswagen, intending to ask the older woman what displays she wanted to see. Before she could ask, several young people nearby caught sight of Aunt Mae and eagerly converged upon her. "Miz Sawyer, hey, great to see you . . . you look wonderful . . . we've missed you."

Aunt Mae caught Leslie's bemused eye. "Some of my former students," she twinkled, obviously touched at their interest. "Why don't you stroll around for a while on your own? I guess I've got some catching up to do."

"Take your time." Leslie waved and turned the stroller toward the tent marked "Homemade Jellies and Preserves." She stopped short when she caught sight of Steven leaning against one of the outside tent poles. He was watching her over the heads of the crowd.

She met his grave gaze steadily, but the color was already rising to her cheeks. There were moments when Steven made her feel extremely vulnerable, and this was certainly one of them. What was he doing here, disturbing her hard-won peace? And what was the matter with *her*? Surely he had a right to visit the fair, too. Wasn't it possible for them to remain civil and friendly to each other?

Knowing Steven, she truly doubted it, but as he came toward her, she decided to try. "Hello," she smiled brightly. "I didn't expect to see you here."

"When no one was at the farm, I assumed you might be here," he explained. "And you got Aunt Mae out of the house, too. Good for you."

Flustered by his unexpected approval, Leslie began to stammer. "Aunt Mae's much more enthusiastic about everything and very busy, too . . . I mean, not *too* busy."

Oddly, she suspected that Steven was about to laugh, but instead he put a warm hand on her shoulder. "You look like a genuine farm girl with that ponytail. But I'll bet this is your first time at a mountain fair. Would you like a guide?"

"I . . . I would like it very much," she responded, pleasantly surprised.

"Then let's go. There's lots to see."

There certainly was. They strolled from exhibit to exhibit, looking closely at the weaving, the pottery, carvings and wood sculptures, everything done with natural materials, all telling stories of a rich and varied heritage. There were watercolor paintings of the hills, simple yet exquisite. There were local foods for sale: sorghum molasses, black walnut preserves, hickory-nut cakes and green-apple pies. Leslie was especially fascinated with the gemstones that were cut into patterns or mounted whole. "The entire Kentucky, Tennessee, Carolina area is rich in gems and minerals," Steven explained. "You could actually go mining on your own in one of the caves and find a ruby; people have done it. Gem crafters use them in a variety of ways."

"They're beautiful." She swung shining eyes to Steven. "Such treasures."

He was watching her evident enjoyment with an interest of his own. "I'm glad you like it all," he said. "I had thought . . ."

"Yes?"

"Oh, it doesn't matter." His light gaze held hers for a moment, and then Penny broke the spell, obviously getting ready to fuss.

"It's time for her to eat," Leslie said, looking at her wristwatch. "I suppose I ought to check on Aunt Mae, too."

"She's still holding court over by the parking lot," Steven assured her. "Why don't we find a quiet spot and take care of the baby?"

She had thought he would leave eventually, but once again she found herself puzzled at his unexpected friendliness. She was determined to enjoy it this time. Wasn't she already discovering that although Steven's flashes of temper were frequent, he was also a person who tried to make amends?

They found a shady picnic table out of the stream of traffic, but close enough that the occasional passerby still noticed Steven and was able to greet him. This had been happening all day, Leslie realized; so many of those attending the fair knew Steven and showed such delight in spending some time with him. He had apparently performed medical services for many of them, for Leslie overheard him inquire about someone's pneumonia and watched as he carefully examined a child's once-fractured arm. At other times, however, he simply enjoyed the warm comradery, his eyes bright with interest, occasionally laughing easily with the others.

"I think I owe you an apology," Leslie murmured as she bent over Penny to feed her.

"Really? That's an interesting idea." Steven stretched leisurely next to her. She could sense how relaxed and contented he was.

"You don't have to make it even harder," she teased, avoiding his eyes. "I once accused you of being a snob and just working to make a lot of money. Remember?"

"Yes. That day we met at the clinic."

"Well, I was wrong," Leslie admitted. "The people here love you, and it's obvious that you've been very good to them too. That kind of loyalty doesn't happen by accident— oh, I'm saying it all wrong!"

"Not at all. I appreciate that." Steven watched her as she spooned strained applesauce into Penny's eager mouth. "I think we've both made some errors in judgment, don't you?"

"Well, yes." She swallowed. "But I'm trying *not* to judge others, Steven. We're supposed to forgive instead of judge, you know, and then we'll be forgiven. . . ."

"And do you have so much to be forgiven for?" His close scrutiny was making her nervous.

"Of course I do!" She tried to remain calm. "Don't you?"

Steven looked taken aback for a moment. "Well, I try to obey the tenets of my faith, to act on my beliefs," he mused thoughtfully. "I suppose you'd say I'm lacking in that extra dimension, that compassion that you find so important. I admit it; I find it difficult to love . . . everyone."

"Compassion doesn't require that you agree with another, or approve of that person's behavior," Leslie pointed out. "It just means that you try to put yourself in his place, feel his pain, do what you can to alleviate it."

"Even if you're angry about that pain?" Steven demanded. "Even if you believe the person brought it on himself?"

"Especially then. Jesus said that if we love those who love us and are acceptable to us, it's no accomplishment. But loving those who are somehow our enemies—that's the way we must love if we want to follow Christ."

She thought he would lash out at her with an angry rebuttal but instead, to her surprise, he smiled. "Pretty good advice. How did you get so wise, Leslie Bennett?"

Leslie shrugged and dipped the spoon into Penny's applesauce. "My grandmother taught me a lot. But I'm not wise, Steven, not wise at all." She thought of the mess she'd made of everything, the dread that never really left her; and the irony of her lecture to Steven became painfully obvious. If Jesus wanted her to love and forgive her enemies, then how could she justify stealing Tony's daughter from him? If being a Christian meant walking in truth, then how could she be such a fraud? She was living a life that was a lie in every way.

Except one. The feeling growing within her was new to her, and although common sense told her she should fight it, she found that she was unwilling to do so. Steven was so handsome, and she felt drawn to the strength that could protect as well as injure. Why did she feel this intense awareness of him as a man when at no time had he been anything more than remotely polite—or angry—with her? And yet something about him sent shivers along her spine.

She looked up and found his light gaze fastened upon her. "Tell me," he said, "do you ever think of Penny's father?"

"Tony?" The question was so unexpected that she was thrown off balance. "Oh yes. I think of Tony every day." *In fear*, she could have added, but at that moment Cindy bounced up to join them, followed by her little boys and a tall sunburned man who looked like a younger version of Jed. "There you are," she beamed. "Leslie, this is my husband, David. And, Steven, stop scowling long enough to give me a hug—it's been ages."

Steven was indeed scowling, Leslie noted, hoping it had nothing to do with her, but in the flurry of activity she put the concern aside. The Parkers were leaving the fair early to go home and check on Jed, then start the barbeque grills. Leslie, Aunt Mae, Steven, and anyone else was invited to go along. Steven, after giving Leslie a long evaluating look, accepted the invitation and walked off with David. Leslie, shrugging, gathered Penny's things and went back to load up her car. Honestly, did Steven have to be so abrupt?

But that was his way, at least with her, and she had to accept it. Besides, what difference did it make? Her primary job, after all, was to stay out of his way, despite her deepening feelings for him. How terrible if he were to discover how she felt! His contempt for her would know no bounds.

She collected Aunt Mae from her crowd of young admirers, several of whom promised to pay a visit to the farm soon, and eventually found her way to the Parkers'. The house itself was much smaller than Aunt Mae's, although it was also better cared for, but the property had the same homey quality. People were already scattered about the wide front lawn, knotted in talkative groups, and Leslie realized, with a sense of happy belonging, that she knew some of them. Paul Ellis and his mother waved to her, and one of the Carney girls came over to explain that Ellen, although still bruised, was doing fine. Steven, of course, was surrounded by friends, and there was Jed sitting comfortably under a shady tree, obviously enjoying all the activity. She pushed Penny's stroller across the grass to his chair and took his gnarled hand in hers. "My favorite little nurse," he smiled in recognition. "What a treat to discover that you're living only a stone's throw away."

"Now that you're home, I'll be over to visit," Leslie promised. "And I brought someone to see you, too."

"Mae." Jed looked past Leslie to where Aunt Mae was standing almost shyly. "Well, isn't this wonderful." Leslie didn't know which one of them appeared more delighted, but she quickly pulled a lawn chair next to Jed's and ushered Aunt Mae into it, casually strolling away as the two of them struck up an animated conversation.

"Nice work!" Cindy observed from the porch. "I've been playing matchmaker for those two for years and haven't gotten anywhere. Maybe you'll have better luck."

"I think they're both just shy, despite all that stomping and snorting," Leslie grinned. "Need some help in the kitchen?"

"No, everything's temporarily under control." Cindy came down the stairs, looking thoughtful. "But I did hope to talk to you about something important. Can we go where it's private?" She led the way to a group of leafy ash trees overlooking a small creek and sank down on the grass.

"What a heavenly spot." Leslie sat beside her.

"Good for fishing. Use it anytime," Cindy invited.

"Leslie, there's no point in beating around the bush. News about Dotty has traveled fast, and everyone's also heard about you and Aunt Mae taking her in. We think you're both wonderful. And . . . there's another girl in the same predicament as Dotty, but her pregnancy is much farther along. She lives way on the other end of town, but things are very hard at home and . . . well, I was wondering if Margaret might come to live with you, too."

"Another one?" Leslie's mouth fell open.

"She's a good hardworking girl," Cindy plunged on, "and David and I would have her here except that we only have three decent bedrooms, and Jed needs extra care right now."

"Cindy, if I asked Aunt Mae, I'm sure she'd say yes, but . . ." She stopped. How could she tell Cindy about her own precarious position, about Steven's threat to throw her out if she didn't obey his orders?

But there was another distraught girl to think of, too, someone who needed help as badly as Dotty, and Leslie sensed that God was asking her to respond. *"Today, if you hear his voice, do not harden your hearts."* She had read the verse only last night, but how appropriate it was now.

She looked at Cindy in resignation. "Of course Margaret can come if Aunt Mae agrees."

Cindy threw her arms around Leslie. "Oh, you're great! I knew you'd say yes! And we'll help you, we all will. We'll bring food and bedding, and the men will move furniture if you need it."

"Cindy, this is only temporary, you know. Steven wants Aunt Mae to sell the farm as soon as possible, and when that happens—"

"We'll just trust God, Leslie. He'll show us what He wants. He always does."

Cindy's simple faith spoke volumes, and Leslie felt

ashamed of her own fears. Quickly she rose. "It's getting late. Let's get dinner on."

They worked together, along with other women who smiled shyly at Leslie when they were introduced, and included her in their cheerful conversation. Outside on the lawn, hamburgers disappeared as soon as they were grilled, along with mountains of salad and gallons of lemonade. An occasional fiddle and banjo joined in a variety of tunes, and people sang along at random.

Leslie loved it all, despite the fact that Steven seemed to be avoiding her. He had said nothing to her all evening, and now she felt in need of a quiet break. Aunt Mae had fed Penny, so Leslie tossed her apron aside and walked alone back to the small creekside area on Cindy's property.

She leaned against an ash tree and watched as the sun sank behind the hills. There was so much to enjoy here, so much to catch at her heart. Kentucky, "land where we will live tomorrow." But it was not her land, and she must never allow herself to forget it.

A twig snapped behind her, and she turned, surprised to see Steven coming toward her. He was barely visible in the fading twilight, but involuntarily she trembled. What now? Had Cindy told him about Dotty or the other young mother-to-be?

Apparently not, for he walked casually over to where she stood. "I'm driving back to Cincinnati now. Just came to say goodbye."

"Oh. You're going tonight?"

"Yes, I am . . . honoring my vow."

Leslie blushed. Did he have to keep reminding her of the promises they had made to each other? She didn't want to remember how she was breaking hers.

Steven stood for a moment and gazed at the hills. "Beautiful, aren't they?"

"Yes, they are. I never get tired of looking at them.

They change, you know. Sometimes they're happy, and sometimes . . ."

She stopped, aware that she was chattering again.

"You love it here, don't you?" Steven looked down at her. "That's something I never anticipated when I hired you."

"What do you mean?" A warning note sounded in her mind.

Steven ran a frustrated hand through his hair. "It . . . this situation . . . it isn't working out at all the way I thought it would. Nothing fits. It's almost as if—"

"What do you mean?" she asked in alarm, and then the pieces fell into place. He was dismissing her. Because, somehow, he *had* found out about Dotty. Or she had done something wrong in another way—but he couldn't! He couldn't just brush her aside like an annoying gnat, just because it suited him. Could he? Anger and fear mingled, rising to fever pitch and, unthinking, she turned and grasped his sleeve. "Steven, please . . ." The unshed tears burned her eyes and throat. "You can't!"

His brows rose in wary surprise, his body tensing as if to ward off a physical blow. "Leslie, what are you talking about?"

His forearm was hard beneath her fingers, the muscles taut, the warmth of his skin perceptible through the soft cotton. She clung to his sleeve as if to a lifeline. "Don't, please don't!"

"What in the world—" He gripped her shoulders firmly. "Leslie, calm down!" Their eyes met and the same tension she had noticed before reappeared. Then Steven's tight control seemed to snap as he muttered something under his breath and pulled her to him. "Leslie," he said once more, and then bent and kissed her.

Her heart felt ready to burst.

Suddenly reason returned and she began to struggle

like a captured bird. "Steven, don't!" She tried to elude him, to break free before her feelings overwhelmed her once again.

"Hush. It's all right." Gently now, as if to soothe a terrified child, he tried to hold her, but she pushed him away, far more fearful of her emotions than his. "No, don't!" she stammered. "This . . . this isn't part of my job!"

The warmth faded completely from his eyes, leaving a bleakness which she endured with lifted chin, her fists buried deep in the pockets of her jeans so he wouldn't notice that they were shaking.

"I see," Steven said finally. He had not moved a muscle, but she had the curious feeling that there was at least a million miles between them now. "You may have given your favors to Lee and Tony and all the others in order to hold a job—"

"That's a beastly thing to say!"

"But you don't have to do it for me. I don't expect that kind of . . . duty from my employees."

Then he hadn't intended to fire her? She looked at his still profile in despair. How could she explain that he was completely mistaken, that she had never allowed a man to kiss her as he had. Her reason finally prevailed, and she turned away, swaying slightly.

His arm shot out to catch her. "Are you all right?" he asked sharply.

"Of course." Her tone matched his except for a slight breathlessness she strove to cover. "It . . . it was only a kiss, after all. And as you say, I've had so many of them."

She tossed her head and turned down the now-darkened path. It was no use. He had judged her once again and found her wanting. But this time she would do everything in her power to keep him from learning the truth. For whatever else this day had taught her, it had revealed one certain thing. She was in love with Steven—hopelessly, desperately in love with him—and nothing had prepared her for that.

10

*T*he outing had done Aunt Mae a world of good, Leslie decided. It was obvious to everyone who saw her during the next few weeks that she had regained much of her zest for life. She and Jed Parker chatted on the telephone like giggly teenagers, and jars of Aunt Mae's blackberry preserves, accompanied by a loaf of her corn bread, were delivered to his door. Aunt Mae went into town with Leslie, visited the tiny branch library on her own, and exchanged *The Case of the Boring Bookworm* (which Dotty had also solved) for *The Case of the Corpulent Colonel*. In addition, she popped in at the yard goods store and stocked up on extra supplies for the students who had taken to dropping in at unannounced hours. "They might as well do something productive while they're chatting with me," she told Leslie briskly. "Even the boys could probably learn to knit scarves—and the good Lord knows their families can use them when winter comes."

Leslie rationalized the idea by telling herself that Steven had only forbidden Bible classes. He hadn't said anything about knitting classes, but the excuse sounded weak even to her. However, who could oppose the bloom in Aunt Mae's cheeks, the enthusiasm even more precious because it had been so unexpected? Aunt Mae had suddenly found herself needed and appreciated, and that had been what was missing all along.

The passing days brought another major event, Dotty's

move into the house and, a short time later, Margaret joining the family. Margaret appeared on the porch one morning, clutching a battered canvas bag, painfully thin except for her large middle, wearing patched soiled clothing and a defeated expression. Aunt Mae loved her on sight. Within hours Margaret had luxuriated in a bubble bath, her lank hair had been trimmed and styled, and she was happily cleaning up the attic room assigned to her.

In their usual quiet but ubiquitous manner, the local people also took part in Aunt Mae's and Leslie's project. Ed Carney arrived one morning and moved a desk from the attic into the empty parlor on the first floor, which Leslie had decided to set up as an office. Ed had an infected finger, and after treating it Leslie announced that she might as well hold occasional clinic hours in the office, too, in case any of the neighbors had the sort of minor bumps or ailments she could soothe.

An unexpected load of day-old bread and dented can goods was left on the porch, along with a note from Mr. Potts, the grocer: "Heard about all the help you're giving us. Will send some extras from time to time. Hope the cats are fine."

Leslie also contacted the closest social service agency, just to make sure Dotty and Margaret weren't missing out on any help. The woman in charge agreed that they should have prenatal exams as soon as possible and perhaps some counseling, too, but felt sure they were in good hands. "In fact," she confided to Leslie, "if you could consider another girl . . . I've been trying to find a place for her. She's a runaway who really needs some love right now."

To almost no one's surprise, Rosalie arrived a few days later in the Grimes family's pickup truck. Mrs. Grimes had been on her way to ask Leslie about a bunion that was troubling her and to drop off some used maternity clothes for the girls at the same time. Rosalie was amazed to discover that Aunt Mae's house came equipped with a real baby, and although she found it difficult to speak to any of the adults, she took over much of Penny's care with a gentleness that belied her rough street-wise exterior.

Paul Ellis and his brother came by to meet everyone and to donate a load of potatoes from the Ellis farm. He mentioned to Leslie that one of the townspeople had been in Covington recently and had met a man who thought he remembered Leslie from Minneapolis.

Leslie dismissed the news, treating it as she treated almost everything these days, from inside a bemused fog. A part of her, of course, remained alert, watching Aunt Mae, the baby, and the girls with an almost clinical detachment. But there was another part of her that functioned on a separate wavelength, the part that was now an awakened woman, incapable of handling anything except the thought of Steven. Over and over she replayed the moment they had kissed. She tried to tell herself that it must be her total lack of any previous experience that made her remember the scene in such minute detail. But she knew that it was more. She had never felt this kind of weakness before. She had always been in control of her emotions. Until now.

Now, one disturbingly tender look, one kiss from Steven had been enough to devastate her. And his subsequent anger had torn her heart to shreds. Over and over again she told herself that she had done the right thing continuing the false impressions she had created, but the words sounded hollow and unconvincing.

And yet, what did any of it matter? She would see Steven only once more, whenever he visited the farm again to dismiss her. He had the upper hand now as always, and he would not hesitate to use it. Despite his unexpected embrace, he was the same harsh and judgmental person he had always been. Leslie was learning the hard way that sometimes you loved someone in spite of what he was, and not because of it.

The Saturday came when she was to take Penny into St. Luke's to have the last set of casts removed, and the entire household gathered in the clearing to see her off. Leslie had originally planned to bring Dotty, Margaret, and Rosalie along for prenatal checkups—it bothered her that none of them had been seen by a physician—but the Volkswagen could never have accommodated everyone, and she hated to leave Aunt Mae alone for a whole day. In the end, she had decided to ask old Dr. Klein from the next county to stop by at his convenience, and had instead packed the car with Penny's things.

Fortified with hugs and kisses, they set off on the long drive. The baby fussed for a while; she was getting almost too big for her car seat, but, lulled by the smooth rhythm, she eventually settled down for her afternoon nap.

Penny was too big for almost everything, Leslie reflected wryly, as the ribbon of highway unfolded before her. The baby would be sitting up soon, so she'd need a highchair, and perhaps a playpen. She had outgrown all her clothes, too. Leslie glanced down at her own outfit, a dated but softly tailored shirtwaist dress, and smiled. Both of them needed new wardrobes and a lot of other things, but mindful of Penny's doctor bill, Leslie had been afraid to spend money on anything but necessities. She had no idea how much the orthopedist would charge, but she would pay it all today if she could and hope there would be time left to accumulate a little bit for car repairs before she took to the road again.

The thought of leaving Kentucky—and Steven—hit her in the hollow of her stomach, and she prayed fervently that she would not run into him today at St. Luke's. It seemed unlikely. Her late-afternoon appointment was in the outpatient wing, far away from surgery, and unless there was an emergency, Steven should be finished at this time of day with both operations and rounds. She regretted that she would not be able to visit Mrs. Ames and catch up on hospital news, but it was too risky a venture—what if she *did* see Steven? Mrs. Ames had never known of Penny's existence anyway, and Leslie didn't feel up to explaining the whole thing. St. Luke's was part of her old life. She need visit it only once more, and that episode could come to an end.

The Volkswagen almost stalled twice on the long hot drive, and it was after four-thirty when she finally reached Outpatient. Leslie was dismayed to find that the orthopedist had been called out on an emergency consultation, and Penny's X-rays had been mislaid. "Go have a cup of coffee," the sympathetic receptionist suggested to Leslie. "We'll get all this straightened out in just a few moments."

Instead, Leslie held the baby on her lap in the waiting room and fidgeted. Ill at ease about meeting Steven and concerned over the bill, she found herself also worried about driving back to Aunt Mae's in the dark, in a car that was badly in need of repairs. As she glanced out the window at the suddenly blackened sky and heard the first distant roll of thunder, her apprehension grew. One bottle of formula in her bag and a couple of extra disposable diapers—what a time to be stranded, perhaps on the side of a washed-out road, with a baby!

Suddenly, part of a verse Leslie had memorized years ago came to her mind: "Surely, I am with you always. . . ." A sense of guilt overcame her as she realized that she couldn't worry about everything and be trusting the Lord at the same time.

Switching Penny to her other arm, she silently prayed, *Lord Jesus, forgive me for not remembering that you are always with me. I need you now, as I always have, and I'll try to trust you more and stop worrying.*

Leslie did feel better about things after turning to her source of life for help. He gave her a sense of peace that had been missing from her life lately.

It wasn't long after this that the orthopedist, Dr. Sanderson, returned amid a flurry of apologies. "Good thing you're a nurse, Mrs. Bennett." He shook his head as he laid Penny on the examining table. "At least you understand about medical interruptions."

"Oh yes," she smiled. Now that the doctor was actually *here*, Leslie found her spirits rising even more.

Dr. Sanderson snapped X-rays up on the wall. "And then, of course, my wife just phoned to remind me that I'm already late for the hospital dinner dance. Should have been home getting dressed an hour ago."

"There's a dinner dance tonight?"

"Yes. A fundraiser for the new street clinic, a very good cause. I hear it's a sellout crowd. Over at the Page Hotel." He squinted at the X-rays, and perused Penny's chart again, then reached for the cast saw.

Leslie felt suddenly lightheaded with relief. Steven would surely be at the dinner dance now, not lurking around the hospital halls. And if he was indeed going to be named administrator of the clinic, he would probably be the evening's guest of honor. In fact—her stomach suddenly trembled at the thought—Steven and Rita might even use tonight's festivities as a means of announcing their engagement. Why not? All the beautiful people would be there and . . . she found that she was incapable of thinking about it.

Instead, she looked at Penny in time to see the last pieces of cast fall away, revealing spindly but very straight legs. "A good job, if I do say so," Dr. Sanderson beamed.

"Oh, they do look wonderful," Leslie enthused. Penny moved a knee and her lips puckered. Leslie laughed. "Look, she knows something's different, and she doesn't like it."

Dr. Sanderson smiled, too, as he gave Leslie detailed instructions about exercise and follow-up care, then moved to the door. "I don't mean to race out this way, Mrs. Bennett, but . . ."

"Yes, I know. The dance. But your receptionist has gone home, Doctor, and I'd like to pay Penny's bill now, or at least part of it."

"Her bill?" Dr. Sanderson frowned and went into the outer office. A moment later he returned, carrying an open file. "Yes, I thought so. Mrs. Bennett, you don't owe anything. The baby's bill has been paid."

"What?" Leslie's mouth dropped. "But . . . by whom? And when?"

"Well . . ." the physician peered at the entry. "It was paid a few days ago, and the code we use indicates that someone on staff here at St. Luke's took care of it."

Steven. And just a few days ago, *after* that disastrous scene at Cindy's barbeque. *Why?* Her chin lifted. Because he felt guilty? She couldn't accept anything from him. She would have to repay him, but how?

Leslie parted from Dr. Sanderson with a sincere thank-you, and, lost in thought, dressed a much-lighter Penny and carried her through the corridors to the parking lot exit. But when they approached the door, she saw in dismay that rain streamed from the blackened skies, lit by an occasional flash of lightning, and the parking lot puddles looked deep. It would be foolish to drive a mile or two in a storm like this, much less attempt to reach a farmhouse in the hill country.

Penny, understandably, was reacting to the tension of the day. Her whimpers in Outpatient had developed into full-fledged screams by now, and Leslie was uncomfortably aware of heads turning her way. She had to get out of the building before Penny got any louder or more hysterical. Perhaps if she drove just a short way, the baby would be lulled to sleep. Taking a deep breath, she plunged into the storm, running and slipping across the flooded parking lot.

The cold rain did nothing to improve Penny's disposition. "Hush, little love," Leslie murmured, urging the car's engine to life and steering it out of the lot onto a main thoroughfare. She could see almost nothing through the windshield despite the flapping wipers, and as another burst of thunder clapped above her, the little car actually shook. This was madness, trying to drive in this kind of deluge with a screaming baby complicating the situation—not to mention her own discomfort, her dress soaked and strands of heavy hair sticking to her cheeks. She had almost reached the expressway, hands clenched on the steering wheel, when the Volkswagen died.

It glided to a final stop right at a lighted corner in the midst of a downtown area. Normally it would have been busy, Leslie reflected bitterly, except that tonight everyone else in Cincinnati had the good sense to be indoors. Frantically she pumped the gas pedal, succeeding only in flooding the already-exhausted engine. Now what? She chewed her lip nervously. Penny's screams had dwindled into wrenching, gasping sobs, but Leslie knew the baby was as cold, wet, and miserable as she. And it wasn't very smart to sit in a stalled car with visibility this poor; another vehicle could easily run into them.

She peered out the windshield. Even though she could barely see out it was obvious that, being Saturday night, the downtown department stores were closed. Where could she find shelter for the baby? Could she phone Mrs. Ames? Leslie had no idea where her former supervisor lived, and she could see no cabs around. She really couldn't go anywhere except on foot. And then she realized exactly where she was—less than three blocks from the plush Page Hotel. She had passed it many times on her way to work, and Steven would be there. He could lend her the money or a credit card to pay for a hotel room. Hope surged wildly within her, to be replaced a moment later by discouragement. How could she barge in on a social event of this magnitude and bother Steven on a night that was of major importance to his career?

Once again Penny's cries filled the car. Leslie realized she had no choice. Whatever Steven thought of her, the baby had to be taken care of. Leslie gathered the sobbing little bundle into her arms and flung open the car door.

It was, perhaps, the longest three blocks she had ever walked. Long before she reached the hotel and squished past the surprised doorman, she was soaked completely through to her skin. Her skirt sagged with the weight of the water, flapping awkwardly against her legs; the wind had blown her heavy hair into a sodden red-gold mass. If she'd had a free hand she would have wrung herself out, but both arms were occupied in attempting to soothe Penny, who shuddered hysterically and clutched a strand of Leslie's hair in her fist. The baby's squalls echoed in the carpeted elevator and could even be heard above the orchestra when the doors slid soundlessly open, revealing a reception area and miles of white-covered tables. There were hundreds of gowned and tuxedoed people, and it seemed all were looking at her.

Blushing, Leslie stepped out of the elevator, grateful that most of the onlookers, after a startled glance, moved on. "Penny, hush!" she whispered frantically as her eyes swept the room. Was Steven there?

"May I help you?" A kindly looking maitre d' swept up to her, studiously overlooking her disheveled appearance. "The baby . . . er . . . is quite loud."

"Yes, I'm sorry. Can you find Dr. Steven Sawyer for me?" She wiped the streaming water from her eyes. "It's rather—an emergency."

"Yes, I see. Dr. Sawyer, hmmm . . ." The man moved away and Leslie backed into the shadows of a nearby potted plant. If she could only sink through the floor, or escape to the rest room? But she had no dry clothes for Penny, and how would Steven find her?

Finally he appeared, following the maitre d' across the dance floor, darkly handsome and trim in his formal clothes, seemingly unaware of how many women watched him pass. Joy trembled within her like a fragile bubble. He was here. He would take care of her somehow, she knew it.

"I'm terribly sorry to interrupt," she blurted as he reached her, his surprised gaze taking in her drenched condition and the baby's hysterical thrashing. "I wouldn't have intruded, but my car broke down." Her cheeks burned. "I need a hotel room tonight, and I don't think they'll take a check. I don't have enough cash, and I don't have a credit card. Could you. . . ?"

"Of course. Are you both all right?"

"Yes, but—"

"Then wait right here and I'll get things straightened out." He laid a hand on Penny's copper curls for just a moment, and she seemed to calm down; then he turned and went back across the dance floor.

The crowd seemed to swallow him up, but not before Leslie had caught a glimpse of Rita Marchand, resplendent in a black form-fitting gown, and realized that she and Steven were talking. Of course he would have to explain his brief absence to Rita. It wouldn't look right otherwise, taking one woman to a hotel room while announcing his engagement to another. She hoped she had not put him in an embarrassing position and stepped behind the plant again to survey Rita and her peers.

They were all alike, she thought rather wistfully. Rich young socialites who had been born to their position, totally unaware of any existence except their own. So many things set them apart from Leslie—the way they dressed, the way they all knew one another, the way they spoke and laughed.

No wonder Stephen had been dazzled. For Rita Marchand, in her glamorous gown, was very much one of them.

And oddly, she was coming across the dance floor now, threading her way through clusters of partygoers until she stood in front of Leslie, mocking eyes taking in every inch of her bedraggled appearance. "Mrs. Bennett?" she asked cooly, although she must have known who Leslie was.

"Yes." Taken aback by Rita's obvious and unexpected hostility, Leslie held the baby even more tightly.

"Steven asked me to give this to you." Rita held out a twenty-dollar bill, barely suppressing a smirk. "It should cover the cost of a room."

Leslie recoiled in confusion. The only room twenty dollars would buy in Cincinnati was a cheap hovel in some down-and-out area . . . and suddenly her stomach lurched as she realized what Steven meant. What he was saying to her, with his contemptuous offer, was that she was only suited to the lowest-class accommodations. And to help get the message across, he had sent his jeering fiancée to do the cruel job for him.

Sickened, she turned, clutching the still-crying baby, and bolted for the elevator. She would not be sick, she would not think about this final humiliation, she wouldn't. The elevator door closed behind her, but she could still feel Rita's eyes burning into her back. She would go back to the car, she told herself wildly. Even though her head was beginning to feel light, and her body was starting to tremble with delayed shock, she could make it. It was only natural that the cold and wet would eventually take their toll; it had nothing to do with Steven's repudiation, nothing at all.

She had covered only half the distance to the car, the beating rain causing her to stagger just a little, when a sleek black car pulled up beside her and the window slid noiselessly down. "Get in," Steven's voice commanded from inside the car.

"No!" she gasped, slogging ahead. How could he possibly expect—?

"Don't argue. Get in."

She could hear the rising exasperation in his tone, but she no longer cared. Recklessly she splashed on.

The car halted, and Steven was out of it in a flash. Ignoring the rain spilling on his dark suit, he caught her and Penny up in an iron grasp. "I said, *get in*!" He thrust them roughly against the seat. "Do you want to get pneumonia?"

"Why would you care?" she cried bitterly, her teeth starting to chatter.

Steven slammed the door. "Why would I care?" he repeated irritably. "Why do you think I'm here? You came and asked me for help, and then you ran away."

"Any decent woman would, after that . . . that mortifying . . ." Her voice was rising. "I'm tired of it, Steven. I don't care what you think of me, but you just can't do those things, not anymore!" She started to weep, and as he put out a hand to steady her, she flinched.

Steven stared at her for a moment as if he didn't believe it, then said with immense weariness, "Have I really frightened and disgusted you this much, Leslie? I'm trying to *help* you, if that's possible. What have I done to mortify you?"

"That . . . that awful money—"

"What money?" he demanded. "What are you talking about?"

She drew in her breath. Was it possible that he didn't know, that Rita Marchand had devised such a disgusting ploy all by herself? But why? "Steven, I . . ." Her head felt light again, and a throbbing had started in her temple.

"Never mind," he said, more gently now. "Let's get you and Penny taken care of first, and then we can argue about this . . . this money."

It was all too much to sort out in her exhausted mind. She leaned back, closing her eyes. The car was warm and comfortable, and dimly she realized that Steven had driven away from the hotel rather than toward it. "Where are we going?" she murmured.

"My apartment. It'll be more comfortable than a hotel room."

"Your apartment? But I can't . . ."

"Yes, you can. Relax." Was that amusement in his voice? "I promise that you'll be perfectly safe with me."

She should have objected again, but she was past caring, past longing for anything except the basics: warmth, shelter, and rest. Penny continued to cry wildly, and the throbbing in Leslie's temple deepened. It seemed only minutes before the car had turned smoothly into an underground parking lot, and the roar of the storm was left behind.

Steven switched off the engine and reached for the baby. "Here, I'll carry her. The elevator's right there."

"She's soaked," Leslie murmured. "She'll ruin your clothes."

Steven made a sound of impatience and took Penny out of her numb arms. In one motion he seemed to get out from behind the wheel, come around, and one-handedly lift and support Leslie. She found herself leaning against him as they went up in the elevator, grateful for his strength. And even when he somehow got his key in the lock and switched on lamps illuminating one of the most beautiful apartments Leslie had ever seen, she found that she wanted to go on leaning.

Steven, as usual, wasted no motions. Depositing the still-wailing Penny on a brocade couch, he pulled off his wet jacket and tie, tossed them carelessly on a chair, and rolled up his white sleeves. "Have you got a bottle for Penny?"

"In my bag. But I don't think she can eat, she's so cold and exhausted."

"We'll see." Gently, as if approaching a trapped animal,

Steven came to Leslie, laid his hands on her shoulders, and propelled her across the living room and into an equally opulent bedroom. She stiffened as she caught sight of the huge bed, but Steven's strong fingers kneaded the back of her neck. "Relax," he ordered softly, and once again she caught a hint of humor in his tone. "The bathroom's through there. Get under a hot shower right away. There's a robe that's too big for you in the closet and . . . the doors all lock on the inside."

He *was* laughing at her, but she didn't care anymore. Warmth and comfort beckoned, and she was already in the bathroom before she heard the click of the door behind her.

11

After a long while, relaxed and blessedly warm, Leslie emerged into an empty living room. The absence of sound confronted her first; Penny was lying on her tummy on a soft comforter spread on the floor, sleeping soundly, a trace of milk still ringing her lips. Clad only in a dry diaper, she was covered with a thick, fluffy bath towel. Ingenious, Leslie admitted. One would think Steven had been a father for years. And where was he? She was obviously alone. Of course. He had returned to the dance, his waiting fiancée, his big evening. Well, she couldn't blame him. Once again she had inflicted her foolish problems upon him; he had rescued her and returned to his real life.

She looked around the luxurious room with its stunning picture-window view of the city, the lush furnishings, casual but definitely expensive, the thick carpeting in soft muted tones—and she was ashamed. She and Aunt Mae had no right to expect Steven to give up all these trappings that his hard-won success had bought. Why should he return to a sprawling old farmhouse, a poor country practice, when it had taken him so many exhausting years to shake the dust from his feet? How dare she make him feel guilty?

The phone shrilled from a desk in the corner, interrupting her thoughts. She ran to it on bare feet, catching it up before it woke Penny. "Hello?"

Silence. Then Rita Marchand's brisk tones. "Put Steven on, please."

"Steven isn't here."

"Oh, come now, surely you don't expect me to believe that!" Rita seemed furious. "You may have manipulated him into taking you to his apartment, Mrs. Bennett, but these ridiculous antics . . ."

"Steven is not here, Miss Marchand, truly." Leslie found she had no more patience for hostilities of any kind. "I assumed he went back to the hotel."

"Oh." Somewhat mollified, Rita subsided. "There are people here looking for him, of course. Everyone wants to wish him well."

"For . . . for what?"

Rita laughed indulgently. "Well, I don't think you'd be interested, Mrs. Bennett. Sorry I bothered you."

She hung up abruptly, the click loud in Leslie's ear, and just then a key sounded in the lock and the front door swung open. Steven stood there, holding two large bags from Peterson's restaurant. Once again, a mouth-watering aroma filled the room. Drops of rainwater sparkled on his dark head as he stopped for a moment, taking in her scrubbed appearance, the bathrobe, oversized and floppy. Once again she sensed that he was uncertain of his welcome, braced for almost any reaction from her. Because she could think of nothing else, she blurted, "Rita Marchand just phoned."

"Oh. I suppose I ought to call her back." Steven made no move to do so, however, continuing to watch her warily.

"I thought you had gone back to the hotel," she stammered finally.

"Would you rather I did?" he asked.

"I . . . no." She spread her hands helplessly. "I really can't think of anything nicer than . . ."

"Than Peterson's food?" Steven's eyes suddenly danced with mischief, and in giddy relief she found herself laughing, too.

"Yes, Peterson's. And I hope you brought that heavenly soup again."

"Of course." As if a weight had been lifted from both their shoulders, they cleared the glass coffee table of its magazines and settled themselves comfortably on the floor. The bags yielded a different main course, but the same tomato and noodle soup and aromatic coffee. This time Steven had added some rich chocolate cheesecake as well. It was an absolute feast.

Even better was the atmosphere, light-years removed from the combative attitude at their first shared meal in Leslie's boardinghouse room. Tonight was the opposite side of the coin. Perhaps it was the surroundings, the infant slumbering peacefully nearby, the intimate tap-tapping of rain on the picture window; or perhaps it was the pleasure of simple conversation, two people getting to know each other as if for the first time, as if the difficult past had never existed. Whatever the reason, they found themselves laughing easily, exchanging stories of work experiences and patients, even arguing mildly over the last national election. At one point, as Leslie leaned across the table, her heavy cloud of hair covering her cheeks, Steven smoothed it back, commenting, "I suppose everyone marvels at your hair. That color . . ."

"It's a family trait." Leslie spoke without thinking. "My mother had it, and my sister, too."

"You have a sister?"

She froze. "I don't want to talk about her," she began, but to her surprise, Steven veered off immediately in a safer conversational direction. It was as if he were gentling her, creating a calm environment that would surround her with peace and security. Gradually, she felt herself letting go of the tensions that had plagued her all day until, leaning back in satisfaction at the end of the meal, she smiled at him. She didn't understand why he had chosen to spend this evening with her instead of Rita, but she did know that Rita, not Steven, had been responsible for the insulting offer of money. "I've enjoyed this," she said. "And I want to tell you how truly grateful I am, not only for you rescuing us tonight but also for you paying Penny's bill. I can't accept that, of course."

"Is that why you were so upset in the car? Because I paid Penny's bill?" She could see him trying to make sense of her outburst.

"Oh no . . . that was just another of our misunderstandings." There didn't seem to be any point in telling him what Rita had done. After all, he loved the woman, and Leslie had no right to gossip about her.

"Well, then, I see no reason why you can't consider the bill paid and the subject closed." Steven smiled at her again. "It's my way of saying thanks for the wise counsel you offered me a while back. It helped me deal with a few decisions in my life."

"My wise counsel?" Leslie was at a loss.

"The idea that unforgiveness can be a block to healing . . . and other things."

"Oh yes, I remember."

Steven leaned back contentedly, arms behind his head. "I figured if you were taking the time to pray for me, I could, too," he explained. "So I asked the Lord to show me who I needed to forgive. And gradually he revealed to me that I was still angry at my parents for leaving me, and at myself for not being able to save their lives."

"Oh, Steven . . ." Once again Leslie caught a glimpse of the grieving youngster within the man beside her. But when he turned to her this time, she also saw the strength.

"You were right, Leslie," he said. "Forgiveness can be a freeing thing. I guess I wanted you to know about it because I'm going to make some changes in my life now, thanks to that."

Her heart sank, but she tried to remain outwardly calm. Would he tell her about his engagement now? "Then the clinic is going to be built?"

"Oh yes, we've managed to get it off the ground."

Why couldn't she come right out and *ask*? Instead, she hedged. "And the new administrator . . . has met all the conditions?"

Steven frowned. "Well, yes. The biggest condition was that no abortions be performed at the clinic. The board of directors is firm about that, and of course, I agree. We thought there'd be a problem with funding because of it, but there wasn't."

"No abortions?" It was not a condition Leslie had expected.

"Absolutely not. There are enough physicians getting rich by destroying unborn babies; we didn't want to add to the carnage." His mouth tightened. "To me, it's a national disgrace. Each baby is a precious gift from God, yet millions are being destroyed because their mothers don't want to be bothered. We consider ourselves a Christian nation, but we tolerate abortion for the sake of convenience." He caught her eye and shrugged wryly. "Sorry for being so honest, but I hate child abuse in any form, and I get pretty steamed up about this subject."

"I can see that," she said, "and I agree with your views. But, Steven, not every woman has an abortion because she's uncaring."

"No?" he countered. "I've seen plenty of them on their third or fourth. They come into the clinic asking if I'll do it—just as casually as having their ears pierced. And then they can go back to their parties and drugs. . . . It's such a terrible waste."

She put her hand on his arm. "I know there are women like that, but I don't think they're the majority. I've worked on pro-life telephone ministries, and I remember many callers feeling pressured into it by their parents or boyfriend, or being so scared because they were alone and couldn't see any alternative." She looked up and found his light blue gaze intent upon her.

"You were alone, but you didn't abort Penny," he pointed out gently.

"Well, no, but that was different." How she hated this masquerade.

"How was it different?"

"I . . . I can't talk about it." And to her astonishment, she yawned!

Steven chuckled softly, then stood and pulled her to her feet. "Come on, sleepyhead; it's time you got some rest," and he walked her to the bedroom door.

If he kissed her again, it would mean nothing, she reminded herself. For hadn't he all but admitted that he was putting down his permanent roots here, with a job change and a wife? There would never be a place for her in his life, and she knew it. Instead, he said, "Sleep well," then turned and walked back into the living room.

It had been a wonderful evening. Sleepily, she tried to bottle and package it in her mind, keep it airtight so she could never lose it.

For that was all she would ever have of Steven—a memory.

———

Leslie awakened at the crack of dawn, a thin shaft of sunlight falling across her face. Despite the hour, she knew by the hollow sound of the apartment that Steven had already gone. Drawing the robe closely about her, she tiptoed into the living room. Penny was still sleeping on the floor, and a folded blanket and pillow on the couch told where Steven had spent the night. She went back and looked into the bathroom. The shower stall was wet, bathmat damp. . .

he had bathed and dressed right here while she slept, and she had never heard him. The thought made her blush, and then she saw the note propped on his dresser:

"Leslie, Emergency surgery. Supplies for Penny in kitchen. Car's been towed and garage will phone. If not, I'll drive you home. Back about ten."

As usual, he had taken care of everything. Alarm seized her as she realized the implications of Steven taking her back to the farm. He couldn't! If he discovered Dotty, Rosalie, and Margaret . . . She sighed. It was not a question of "if," but of "when." She had burned her bridges the day she and Aunt Mae accepted the girls' problems as their own, and there was no turning back. "Well, what else could I do, Lord?" she asked aloud. "What would you have done?" But she knew the answer to that. "Lord, when did we see you homeless and afraid. . . ?"

"Whatever you did to the least of my children you have done it unto me. . . ."

But there was a price to be paid for that answer, and Leslie knew it. *She* would be homeless soon, but if she could keep Steven from discovering that she had blatantly disregarded his instructions, forestall the inevitable dismissal just a little longer. . . .

Her dress had dried and she went to put it on, frowning as she grappled with her dilemma. What garage had her car? And how could she get it and start the drive home alone? It was shortly after she had fed Penny and tidied the apartment that the fortuitous phone call came: the garage was just on the next block, and her car was fixed.

For once, everything was working. She wrote Steven a note, telling him about the car and thanking him for all his help. He'd be glad when he found her gone, she rationalized. Surely he would want to spend the rest of today with Rita, especially after ignoring her the way he had last night. They obviously had a rather peculiar relationship, but Leslie found that when she thought about it, her throat constricted and her eyes grew moist. There was no point in that. Instead, after a last glance around the apartment, she hoisted Penny into her arms and trudged to the service station.

It was after she had written a check for the repairs and put Penny in the car that she realized everything was not working, after all. Steven's big black car glided to a stop right next to hers and, lean and jean-clad for a day in the country, he came up to her car. "How about some coffee?" he asked conversationally.

"I . . . I think not," she stammered, quickly trying to get her key in the ignition.

Effortlessly, Steven reached in and took the keys from her shaking fingers. "I think so," he told her, his tone brooking no argument.

Unwilling to argue, she followed him to the vending machine, not daring to meet his eyes as he placed the coffee cup in her hand. Finally he put a finger under her chin and raised her troubled face to his. "Will you tell me," he asked wearily, "why you are always running away from me? Have I hurt you that badly?"

"Oh no. I thought you'd be glad not to have to take me to Aunt Mae's."

"I was planning on going anyway. I told her that last night on the phone. It's something else, isn't it?"

"No, Steven, nothing." Panic rose. He was going to the farm today!

"Look, I don't blame you for feeling the way you do about me," Steven sighed. "I've been pretty rough on you, judging you the way I have. But I've discovered that you *are* trustworthy, Leslie. You've taken care of Aunt Mae the way I asked you to, despite our disagreements, giving her a calm atmosphere. . . . Leslie, what's the matter?"

She knew she had gone pale, and she had to dissuade him, whatever it cost. "Steven," she blurted, "didn't we have an agreement? Didn't you promise to leave me alone?"

He was taken aback. "Yes, I did."

"Then do it! Just give me my keys and let me go—alone."

Steven stared at her for a moment, his face turning hard and watchful, before dropping the keys in her outstretched hand, then striding to his own car without a backward glance. She felt a rush of tears and steeled herself against them. If she gave in, if she ran to him and begged forgiveness for her hostility. . .but that was foolish. She had bought some time for herself, Penny, and the girls, and the price was worth it.

She told herself that, all the way to Aunt Mae's farm while the ache in her throat threatened to burst.

It was not until she turned into the driveway, bumping her way through the ruts, that she realized she had not paid the price at all. For coming over the rise, just far enough behind her to have gone unnoticed, was Steven's big black car.

It was, she reflected later, the worst of all possible ways for Steven to learn the truth. If she had had the courage to prepare him, or if Aunt Mae had known of his objections and softened the blow somewhat, it wouldn't have been so shocking. He pulled up next to Leslie, sitting helplessly in the parked Volkswagen, got out, and stood for a moment looking at the porch. There were at least five teenagers sitting on the sagging steps, and a couple of younger boys, too, one without a shirt. Aunt Mae, sitting in the midst of the admiring circle, was mending the shirt while talking earnestly to the youngsters at the same time. The others all held knitting projects in varying stages of completion, and were good-naturedly teasing one another about their skill. The radio was tuned to a Christian church service, and the gentle beat of gospel music wafted out into the clearing.

"Who," Steven muttered under his breath, "are all

these kids, and why are they disturbing Aunt Mae like this?"

Leslie couldn't answer him. Aunt Mae, however, did not look in the least disturbed. Lifting her head, she caught sight of the two cars. "Steven! Leslie! You came home together, how lovely. Come and see what we're doing here."

At that, the screen door opened and Dotty, in a maternity smock, bounced out. "Dr. Steve! Oh, great—it's been ages since we've seen you!" Beaming, she came toward him, and Leslie saw the shocked look on his face.

"Dotty, you're expecting a baby?"

"Didn't Leslie tell you? I thought she brought you home to give us our prenatal exams." She put an arm comfortably through his. "Come and meet the others."

"What . . . others?" Stunned, Steven allowed himself to be led to the porch while Dotty continued to chatter brightly. "It was all Leslie's doing," Leslie heard her explain. "If it wasn't for her . . ."

She sat in the car for a moment or two longer, praying earnestly for an earthquake or maybe a small tornado, watching Steven go up the porch stairs, embrace Aunt Mae and meet Rosalie, who came down to Leslie's car and wordlessly collected the baby. Then weary and defeated, and with no tornado in sight, Leslie climbed out of the car and trudged up the walk. Most of the teens were leaving now that Aunt Mae was otherwise occupied, but there was still a bit of congestion in the front hall near the right-hand parlor.

"And Leslie turned this room into a sort of examining room-office," Aunt Mae explained, motioning to the desk and the old kitchen table, covered with a white cloth. "Isn't she clever?"

"I see." Steven's eyes, still dazed but turning wintry, met Leslie's across the heads. "And is Leslie practicing medicine here?"

"Oh, of course not," Aunt Mae chuckled. "It's just first

aid, Steven. Where else can the people go? And as for Dotty, Margaret, and Rosalie . . ."

"Yes," Steven said. He had become very quiet. "Tell me about the girls, Aunt Mae. Was this . . . boardinghouse Leslie's idea, too?"

"Well, somewhat." Aunt Mae put an affectionate arm around him. "We'll explain it all, darling. I assumed Leslie had filled you in. But right now, as long as dinner isn't quite ready, could we prevail upon you to give the girls their checkups? Dr. Klein still hasn't been out, and—"

"Of course," Steven said smoothly. Only Leslie heard the steely undertones. "I'd be glad to."

As if in a fog, she went to the closet and took out a starched white lab coat. Meekly, she handed it to him.

"Very professional," he said under his breath.

"Steven, I . . ." She found it impossible to look at him.

"Now I understand why you tried to keep me from coming out," he said. "You lying little . . ."

Turning, she fled up the stairs.

12

$\mathcal{S}$he didn't come down for dinner, claiming exhaustion from the long drive, but in reality Leslie was planning her departure. She sensed that she was the one who held the others together, and wondered what would become of them when she was gone, but it was not her decision to make. It had never been her decision—not really.

Margaret came upstairs, bringing her a bowl of soup and the news that David Parker had met someone in town who seemed interested in getting in touch with Leslie. "An older man, I think," Margaret reported. "About thirty."

"Thanks, Margaret. You're great for the ego." Leslie grinned in spite of herself. "Probably someone else with a pregnant girl who needs a place to stay."

"Oh, that would be nice," Margaret smiled shyly. "I mean, not so nice to be in trouble, but . . . good to be with people who love you even if you are."

Leslie was moved. "Why, thank you, Margaret," she said, feeling her throat close up. Margaret was so young, so vulnerable. Who would care for her when . . .

She read Gram's Bible for a while as she often did, absently tracing the roughly mended lining with her finger, waiting for consolation or at least some insight on how to deal with her problems. But nothing came, except the knowledge that she had lied, and that, as Steven had once told her, people who violate the rules do get hurt.

Eventually, she began to take her belongings out of the bureau drawers and stack them in piles for packing. How was she going to tell Aunt Mae? Perhaps Steven had already done that, or was, even now, sending the girls away too. But he couldn't! Sudden anger flared at the thought of their fate, and Leslie found herself on the stairs, marching firmly down to the porch. The house was quiet, but as she pushed open the screen door, she saw Steven sitting deep in thought, feet propped on the porch rail, chin in hands. Quietly she went and sat down next to him. He didn't look at her, but she sensed the tautness in him and realized that as he had sometimes gentled her, it was now her turn to soothe him.

"Rosalie was a street child, a throwaway who, I suspect, had been abused by her stepfather," Leslie began softly. "She still flinches if you make a sudden move around her, but caring for Penny and living with people who don't hurt her is helping her to value herself.

"Margaret was raised in poverty. This is the first bed she's ever slept in. But now she's learning about nutrition and hygiene, and also learning that she's smarter than she thought she was. I think Margaret's going to make it.

"And Dotty. Dotty was a girl looking for love in the wrong places. Her father is starting to accept her, and she's probably going to give her baby up for adoption and go to college and major in Home Ec."

Steven lifted his head. "Home Ec?" he echoed incredulously. "Dotty?"

"Well, maybe it all won't fit, but she has to hope, Steven. Someone had to give her some hope."

"It's not enough, don't you see?" Steven's voice was rough. "It'll never be enough to stem the tide. Three girls here, but thousands who are homeless, aborting their children . . . it's all too big for us."

"Maybe. But I remember reading something about Mother Teresa of Calcutta. Someone asked her why she didn't get discouraged when she looked at the vast problems of India. She said that she didn't look at the vast problems. She just looked at one person at a time."

Leslie broke off, but Steven remained stubbornly silent. She took another deep breath. "Aunt Mae and I talked it over, and we decided that it wasn't enough for a Christian to just be for or against something. Following the Lord means *doing* something, putting our faith to work, you see."

"Oh, spare me the hypocrisy," Steven answered bitterly. "Where was *your* faith? Couldn't you at least have told me what was going on here?"

Leslie bit her lip. "I have no excuse for that. Except to admit that I'm not a very brave person."

"On the contrary, I'd say you were extremely brave, plunging into this crazy scheme, turning my home into a halfway house without a backward glance. And besides," he looked at her grimly, "would it have required that much bravery to level with me?"

She was astonished. "Why, of course!"

"Why?" he demanded.

"Why? Because if you'd known, you would have thrown all of us into the street."

Steven recoiled as if she had slapped him. "Thrown you . . ."

"Oh yes." She rushed on. "There was no question of that. You threatened me, remember?"

"I never intended it as a threat. There were certain things I wanted you to do for Aunt Mae. . . ."

"Well, I failed." She swallowed hard. "And, Steven, even though I don't have any right to ask you . . . if I promise to take Penny and leave this house and never trouble you again, will you let the girls stay, just until their babies are born?"

Steven's mouth was a thin, bitter line. "And I suppose you'll go back to Tony?"

Tony. Surely Steven couldn't think . . .And yet perhaps it would be the safest way to end things, to allow Steven to believe she loved another man rather than him. She looked at him in torment, aware that no matter what happened, her life would never be the same again. She thought of all the lies and prevarications that lay between them, manufactured for her protection, and wished with all the power that was in her that she dared to tell him she was not the person she claimed to be. How would he react? He would be furious, of course, but would he understand her position?

No. The knowledge lay within her like a stone. She had gone too far, and one more lie was needed to end the farce at last.

"Tony," she said slowly, pretending to consider. "Yes, I think I'd like to see Tony again."

"Then go ahead." Steven swung his legs off the porch rail and stood up. "I guess my first impression of you was the right one, after all. Be out of here in a few days, and the girls can stay."

She tried to ignore the disgust in his voice. "Thank you," she said quietly, drawing the remains of her dignity around her like a cloak. "That's very generous."

"Generous!" he muttered in contempt and strode out to his car. "Tell Aunt Mae I've gone," he called across the clearing, then squealed down the rutted drive, scattering gravel in his wake.

She watched until the car had disappeared over the rise, stood motionless long after the sound of it had died away.

The next few days passed in a haze of suffering as Leslie moved through them like a sleepwalker. A terrible sense of loss pervaded her whole being, as if something very precious to her had died. She felt exactly the way she had at Gram's and Lee's deaths, and yet there seemed to be an extra dimension of sorrow here. Something told her that this loss could have been prevented.

It was obvious to the others that she had endured something traumatic, but they were unwilling to pry. And Leslie was equally reluctant to explain it to them. Would Aunt Mae benefit by knowing how Leslie and Steven had hurt each other? Would the girls be contented if they discovered that Leslie had bargained away her own security for theirs? No, it would be wiser to keep it to herself, to ignore their sympathetic glances, to join in the laughter and comradery, at least on the surface.

By Wednesday afternoon she had quietly packed almost everything she and Penny owned, but had not yet approached Aunt Mae. Yet the time was drawing near. Steven had given her just a few days to get out, and she dare not stretch his ultimatum. She would go tomorrow morning.

With that decision made, and the household quieted down for after-dinner rests, she turned for one last walk on her beloved hills. As she walked, her mind buzzed like a bee trapped behind glass, and with the same desperation. It all had to begin again, the frantic flight, the weary search for a roof over their heads and a job and a decent day-care center. Had she *learned* anything from this tragic experience?

Where had she gone wrong? She tried to think logically. Had it been wrong to take Penny out of that sordid Chicago tenement? No, but might there have been a more straightforward way to handle the dilemma? Should she have gotten a hospital job under false pretenses, masqueraded as a parent? What if she had been honest with Steven from the start? How could she be sure that he would have rejected her in her need? She had felt so certain of the answers at the time, but everything she had touched had fallen apart.

For the first time, she realized she had not felt a real moment's peace since she had left Minneapolis. And the loneliness, the inner turmoil, even the times when she couldn't sense the Lord's presence—hadn't it all begun when she took that wrong step in Chicago?

She found the old stump and sank down upon it, filling her soul with scent and fading sunlight and rustling of leaves all around her. "Well, what else could I do, Lord?" she prayed earnestly. "I did what I thought was best. Why did I fail? Please, please help me to find the way."

And softly, almost like a sigh, a delicate breeze kissed her hot cheek, and a gentle voice spoke within her spirit: *I am the way, the truth and the life.*

Oh, Lord, of course! She saw it clearly now as if a veil had been lifted. She had chosen her own way, not God's, when she made the decision to be someone she was not. And as she obscured the truth of her own life, she had found it harder to keep in touch with God's truth, almost impossible to walk in His light. "Oh, Lord, I did it to myself!" she cried aloud. "I tried to convince myself that doing wrong would make things right. But always, there was that little voice inside me, your voice, that kept trying to tell me that you never bless deception. Oh, why didn't I listen? Why didn't I hear you until it was too late?"

The tears now came in earnest. It was no longer possible to hold them back, and there was no one but God to see and understand. She wept for her betrayal of God's laws, knowing that He had loved her through it all and forgave her now. She wept for Penny and Aunt Mae and all the others that she had loved and yet deceived, and somehow she knew that they, too, would understand.

And she wept for Steven, the proud man who might have become a part of her life had she trusted God instead of herself. It was too late now, but she pictured his face and sent a blessing to him wherever he was. "Lord, let Rita love him the way he needs and deserves to be loved."

Finally she wept for herself, a healing, cleansing weeping that left her, at the end, exhausted, still grieving, but with a clearer sense of purpose than she had known for many months.

There would be no more lies. In just a moment she would leave this peaceful place and walk down the hill to Aunt Mae's house, where everyone would surely be looking for her by now. She would confess to the girls and that dear old woman that she was not Penny's mother but her aunt, and she would phone the sheriff in town and ask what he thought she should do. If it meant that Penny would be taken from her and placed into foster care, then she would bow to God's authority in the matter. He was in charge of Penny, had always been in charge, and it was time Leslie acknowledged it.

And Steven. If only she could see him once again. It was impossible, of course, and perhaps the contempt that he felt for her now would deepen by her confession. But she could write him a letter. She could make sure that he knew there had never been a Tony, or any other man, in her life. She could ask his forgiveness for the angry words she had so often hurled at him. However briefly, she had seen some of the wounds he carried, and she was ashamed. A wiser woman would have known how to disagree with him without provoking his pride, adding to his pain.

Maybe she would admit in the letter that she loved him,

had perhaps loved him since the very first time she had seen him.

No. There were some truths that would serve no purpose by being revealed, and this was one of them. If she truly loved Steven, she would give him nothing to feel guilty about. Instead, she would help him close their own chapter completely, so he could start the rest of his life with Rita, the woman he had chosen. Perhaps someday she would even be able to think of him being happy with Rita. But not now. Not yet.

After she had written the letter, well, she and God would decide her next step together. She would need the healing powers of time and prayer to smooth away the jagged edges of her pain, to quiet the part of her that threatened to break loose in an agony of longing. It would be a daily struggle, saying goodbye to Steven, and it would take a long, long time. But she had plenty of time now.

Sighing, she finally stood and brushed off her jeans. The sun was setting, bathing the world in a warm rosy glow. She would carry a part of Kentucky with her wherever she went, and she knew she would weep again when she left. But she was stronger now, ready to do what had to be done.

She turned, took a few steps down the incline, and on the path, saw Steven.

It was as if a bolt of lightning had traveled through her, so stunned was she at the sight of him. In spite of the shock, she felt joy welling up inside. No matter how scornful he might be, she could tell him the truth face-to-face. She had been given a second chance, a miracle! "You've come back," she whispered, scarcely daring to believe it.

"Don't run away," Steven said quietly, "not until I have a chance to tell you something."

Run away? Instead her feet seemed chained to the ground. "I'm so glad you came," she could hear her voice trembling, "because I have things to tell you, too, things I should have told you long ago."

"I'll listen. I promise. But first . . ." He stopped. Leslie sensed his reluctance, could see even in the deepening darkness that he was braced for another quarrel. But however harsh his words might be, she felt no fear now. This was Steven, the man she loved, and no matter what he said or did, she would never hurt him again.

"Go ahead, Steven," she said gently. "I'm listening. I won't run away."

"I can't deny it any longer, Leslie," his husky voice traveled across the distance that separated them. "I can't let you go without telling you that, whatever kind of life you've led, whatever lies you've told, I don't care. I love you."

The ground pitched under her feet. "You. . .you what?"

"I love you," Steven repeated simply. "I never wanted you to leave. That was just my wounded pride talking."

"You . . . you love me?" she echoed faintly.

"I know I haven't been the first man you've cared about, but for a long time I've hoped I could be the last. I know that's pointless because you love Tony, or maybe even Lee, but I kept thinking that if I took a chance and told you how I felt—"

"Oh, stop, stop!" Excitement exploded within her as she covered the distance between them. "You don't have to say any more, Steven." She hurled herself into his arms. "I love you, too. You're my first, and my last, and my *only* . . ."

"Leslie!" He searched her face in disbelief for a moment before the fire leapt into his eyes. Wordlessly he gathered her into his arms and held her as if he would never let her go.

She clung to him, scarcely daring to accept what was happening. Steven loved her! Even believing that she had led a questionable life, he had put aside his judgment of her and accepted her as she was. It was too much to believe.

She felt his hand stroking her hair. "My darling girl," he whispered, "I can't believe you love me. I've hurt you. . . ."

It was her turn to comfort. "I have so much to tell you, Steven, so much hurt of my own to undo."

"I'll listen to it all. But do you think you and Penny could go on loving a stubborn, opinionated man like me for the rest of your lives?"

"Oh, Steven!" Tears of joy sprang into her eyes. "Oh yes, yes!"

"Leslie . . ." he drew her close once more, and as their lips met, a twig snapped in the dusk.

"Very touching," a man's voice broke the silence.

Steven's dark head shot up. "Who's there?" he demanded.

"You wouldn't know me, Doc," the voice came again, and a husky swarthy-looking stranger rounded the curve and came into full view. "But I think the little lady might guess right."

The unfamiliar but somehow sinister tones confused her for a moment, and it was so hard to see his face. But suddenly, with a sinking heart, Leslie realized who their visitor was. "You're Tony, aren't you?" she quavered.

"Tony!" Steven stiffened beside her.

"Yeah. Thought you might figure it out. And there's no doubt in my mind who *you* are. Even in this light, you're the spitting image of Lee, right down to the same shade of hair."

"Yes. People never could tell us apart. I was devastated when I heard of her death, Tony." Leslie spoke calmly, trying to soften an air of menace that seemed to be settling about them. "I miss her terribly, and I know you do, too."

"Lee was your sister?" Beside her, she sensed Steven working out the puzzle.

"Yes," she turned to him. "And Tony was her . . . her—"

"Never mind." Impatiently Tony interrupted. "That's all over now, except for something Lee took from me. You've got it, Leslie, and I came for it."

"No!" Panic-stricken, she gasped. "Don't take the baby, Tony. What sort of life would she have with you? I know you're her father, but Lee wanted me to raise her. And I'll take good care of Penny. Please."

Steven's arm tightened protectively around her, and from the depths of her fear she realized that he knew everything now. She hadn't had to confess anything after all. But had she come so far, gone through so much, only to return Penny to Tony? "Please don't take the baby, Tony." She fought for control.

"I've already got her," Tony announced.

"What!" she screamed, and Steven started forward, fists clenched.

He was stopped in his tracks by the sight of a large pistol, held threateningly in Tony's hand. The last of the sunlight glinted off its silver surface and Leslie's heart began to pound. She had never seen anything so frightening.

"Smart thinking, Doc," Tony said to Steven, who was now standing motionless, eyeing the pistol. "I'm a good shot, and this gun can do a lot of damage. It could shatter both your hands before you knew what hit you. Wouldn't be too good for your practice now, would it?" He laughed shortly.

Leslie felt the bite of nausea. How could a human being even think about maiming another? Steven's relaxed voice reassured her.

"No, it wouldn't, Tony. Why don't you just tell us what we can do for you?"

"Yeah. Now you're making sense." Tony seemed to calm down a little. "First, Doc, you can move farther away from Leslie. I don't want any private signals going on here."

"No problem." Steven moved a few paces to his left. "This about right?"

Leslie looked at him in bewilderment. Far from being intimidated, Steven seemed almost casual, as if he faced a loaded gun every day. He caught her eye and sent her a smile of such extraordinary tenderness that her head nearly spun. He knew, and he understood, and he had forgiven her for it all . . . somehow, nothing else seemed to matter. Except Penny. Where was she? The panic started to rise again, but Steven spoke first.

"I'm curious, Tony," he said. "You say you've taken the baby. But where is she?"

"None of your business," Tony retorted. "But don't worry, she's not in that farmhouse. I took her out of there while everyone was still asleep. The place was wide open."

The lump in Leslie's throat grew. While she had been up here, wallowing in self-pity instead of being a proper guardian, Penny had been stolen from her crib and deposited . . . who knew where? "Is she all right?" she heard herself asking faintly.

"She's okay now. And she will be, just as long as you cooperate."

"But you've got the baby," Leslie said miserably. "What more do you want?"

Tony grinned derisively. "Leslie, use your brain. I don't want Penny. What would I do with a kid? She's just an insurance policy, sort of, to make sure I get what Lee took from me.

"I've thought it all out and spent a lot of time tracking

you down, Leslie, because you're the only one that could possibly have it."

"What is it, Tony?" Steven asked quietly. "What does Leslie have that you want?"

"Why," Tony answered slowly, "she's got the Bible."

Leslie's knees felt weak as she realized she was in the midst of a nightmare that wouldn't end. This terrible man wanted Gram's Bible? Why? To read it and perhaps meditate? As a sentimental keepsake of his dead lover? A hysterical bubble of laughter threatened to escape her lips, but once again Steven's steadiness rescued her.

"I think you can bring Tony the Bible, can't you, Leslie?" Steven asked, and as she turned to face him, she saw the alert gleam in his eyes, and caught a sense of power controlled. Strangely, Steven seemed to know something she didn't.

"Yes, yes, of course I can," she stammered, picking up his cue. It didn't have to be logical; she would honor any demand Tony made in order to save Penny. As she took a step down the path toward Tony and behind him the farmhouse, his next words halted her.

"Wait," he ordered, and she stopped as he tossed what he had been holding in his other hand, a coil of clothesline. It thudded at her feet, and she looked at it with growing dread.

"Before you go anywhere, you're going to tie Doc to that tree over there. And do it right." Tony's voice had lost its conversational tone. He was all business now. "And then you're going to bring the Bible to me. If you do that, I'll put the baby out in a ditch somewhere safe, where someone'll find her. You'll get her back."

"Oh, please, you can't . . ." The sickness was rising in Leslie's throat again, and in just a moment she was going to scream.

"If you don't come back real quick, or if you're dumb

enough to call the cops," Tony went on, "your boyfriend's going to end up with a smashed skull. And even if the cops get me, no one's going to find Penny, not until it's way too late. Get it?"

She met Steven's eyes in horror. "Steven, Penny's going to die!"

"Easy, darling. Don't lose your grip now."

"Hurry up, both of you. Get over to that tree!" Tony commanded.

Leslie looked at the rope, aghast. "Oh, Steven, I . . . I can't do it. He could beat you or . . ."

"It's all right," she saw the alert, watchful expression on Steven's face, and sensed again a strength she couldn't identify. "Do exactly as Tony says. It will all work out, darling. Trust me."

Trust me. Was Steven trying to tell her something? How many times had she refused to trust him, following her own instincts instead? And how often had she made the situation worse instead of better?

It would not happen again. Mutely she stooped to pick up the rope, and as she did so, she heard a sound of running feet. Without warning Steven shoved her into the dirt as he tore past her into the fight, and she went sprawling. There was a shout and another, and more shuffling feet, then a thud and a muffled grunt. The shadowy clearing seemed to be full of people, and as Leslie raised her dazed face, she saw a tangle of arms and legs, then watched as Tony's pistol skittered across the trampled grass. Someone—was that David Parker?—fell upon it. "Got the gun, Steve," Leslie heard him say. "Steady now."

"Everything's okay," she heard another voice report. She saw Steven rising from the ground, breathing hard, and realized that the men had Tony in their custody. It had all happened so fast. Another wondrous event, another miracle that she would eventually sort out, but right now as she got to her feet, she had only one thought in mind. "Penny," she croaked. "Where's the baby?"

"She's okay, Leslie," David Parker reassured her. "Cindy's taking care of Penny at our house. The baby was never out of our sight, not for a minute."

"Penny's safe?" The ground teetered ominously to one side. Steven was already running toward her when, for the second time in her life, Leslie fainted, pitching forward into his arms.

13

"*I* guess you're going to have to explain it rather slowly," Leslie admitted apologetically from the comfort of Aunt Mae's couch. Despite Steven carrying her home and reviving her and ordering her into a warm tub—and Dotty and Margaret fussing over a supper tray, and Aunt Mae plumping pillows and hugging her—her head still felt woolly. Penny nestled comfortably in one of her arms, noisily sucking her sleeve. Steven was sitting on her other side, holding her hand, unwilling to leave her for even a minute. A quiet contentment was beginning to fill her, diminishing the horror of the last few hours.

Aunt Mae's living room seemed full of people, all twinkling at her and Steven with knowing glances, and all, apparently, reluctant to be the first to speak. Finally, Paul Ellis took the initiative.

"See, ma'am, some of us figured that this Tony guy was stalking you. First someone spotted him asking questions in Covington, then Mr. Parker met him in town."

"I didn't like his attitude," David added simply from across the room. It seemed to be reason enough.

"We decided to watch the house every night, just in case," Paul went on. "And tonight he showed up. Mr. Grimes followed him when he took Penny to a hiding place in the fields, only Tony didn't know he was on Parker land. When he left, Mr. Grimes just brought Penny up to the Parker house. Then we kept watching, and we saw what he tried to do to you and Dr. Steve, and we got him." He shrugged and took a huge bite of the bologna sandwich Aunt Mae had made for him. "That's about it."

"But . . . but why?" Leslie asked in bewilderment. "Why would you all give up your sleep, put yourselves out like that, for me?"

Several pairs of eyes dropped in embarrassment; ears reddened and feet shuffled. Finally Ed Carney spoke. "You've been good to us, Miss Leslie. It was our turn to care about you."

It was perhaps the most eloquent testimony to love that Leslie had ever heard. She swallowed hard. "But you took such a terrible chance, all of you. Tony had a gun and . . ."

"That was tricky," Steven admitted. "That's why I kept urging you to cooperate with him, Leslie. I wanted him to stay calm, and I wanted *you* out of the way before the men made their move."

"You knew they were watching?"

"I heard them. Right after Tony appeared."

"But it was so quiet up there."

"Not to a mountain man," Steven smiled. "When you've hunted in those hills all your life, you know every noise. Including the sound of a group lying in wait."

"So that was why you seemed so relaxed." She understood now.

"Well, I was praying under my breath." Steven raised her fingers to his lips and she saw his bruised knuckles, the lines of strain around his eyes. "I'm sorry I pushed you down, but I had no choice. You could have been shot. A lot of things could have gone wrong, for everyone."

Silence descended for a moment as people pondered the sobering possibilities; then Leslie thought of another question. "The Bible?" she asked. "Did Tony really track me just to recover Gram's Bible?"

"Not the Bible," Jed Parker spoke up from a chair next

to Aunt Mae, "but the key that was hidden in it."

"In the back lining, Leslie," Aunt Mae added. "Remember how bumpy the fabric felt? That was because your sister had hidden a key there. The sheriff found it when we showed the Bible to him."

"The Chicago police believe the key will fit a safety deposit box where Tony hid a large amount of cocaine before he went to jail," Jed explained. "Whether Lee put the key in the Bible for safekeeping or whether she was trying to hide it from Tony, we'll probably never know. But when he escaped from prison, he knew he had to find it. That cocaine would have paid his bills for a long time."

"I think Lee might have been trying to save Tony from himself," Leslie said slowly. "I'd like to believe that she found Jesus at the end and tried to make amends for the kind of life she led. Giving me the key—maybe she was passing her concern for Tony on to me." She looked at Steven. "Do you think it would be too ridiculous if—if I sent Tony the Bible?"

"No," Steven smiled. "God can soften any man's heart, can't He?"

"Yes," she smiled back, and a curious sense of peace settled around her, as if Lee were finally at rest. Somehow she knew she would not have the nightmares again.

She looked at the people in the living room in amazement. "You've put it all together so quickly. And here, all this time, I was running for the wrong reason. I thought Tony wanted Penny, not a key."

"The sheriff took the liberty of telling the Chicago police about Penny, too," Steven told her gently. "They'd like you to come up there when you can and do all the paperwork, but the authorities seem to feel that Penny can remain in your custody. After all, Tony's going back to jail, and you're her only other relative. And besides, everyone here is willing to testify that you're a wonderful mother." His eyes warmed with understanding. "Including me."

"Oh, Steven . . ." She dropped her face into her hands for a moment, struggling for control. *Lord, this is too much, all at once.* As she had borne rejection and suffering, she now knew acceptance and joy. A time for everything. A time to mourn, and a time to dance. . . . How truly balanced life could be with its lessons and rewards.

Tactfully the crowd started to disperse. Rosalie confiscated Penny and disappeared toward the rocking chair on the front porch. Margaret and Dotty decided to finish the last chapters of *The Case of the Dilapidated Dumptruck,* while Aunt Mae and Jed, holding hands, left to inspect the moon. Slowly the others came to say goodbye, shyly grasping Leslie's hand for a moment, touching Steven's shoulder in a gesture of silent support. And as the last one left, Leslie's eyes were bright with unshed tears. "I love them," she told Steven. "I'm going to miss them so much when we leave."

"Leave? Why would we do that?" Steven moved to the couch, and put an arm comfortably around her.

"Aren't we moving to Cincinnati?" she asked, confused.

"You'd even give up Kentucky for me? Now I know you love me," Steven teased. "But it won't be necessary, my darling girl. Can't we practice medicine right here?"

"Oh, Steven. Here, in the house?"

"Why not? It's big enough, and we could make it really beautiful. You have the office started and the lab coats stashed. Aunt Mae tells me that there's another pregnant girl that needs a home, and I noticed more cats out in the garage. And from the looks of things, Mae and Jed might make our wedding a double ceremony. Who would want to miss all that excitement?"

"But, Steven, what has changed you?" She was astonished. "You didn't used to feel this way at all!"

Steven grew serious. "Well, Leslie, a man's mind can get muddied sometimes with dreams of power and glory. It's easy to forget that the most glorious thing anyone can do is serve God through His people.

"I guess I lost sight of that for a while. I tried to make it on my own without letting the Lord direct me because I was angry at Him for taking Mom and Dad away. I decided I'd obey Christian rules and maybe even serve the poor, but I'd do it on my terms. I was going to be a hotshot physician in a major medical center, and Aunt Mae was going to share my success with me whether she liked it or not! I was going to control my life, and I wasn't going to get too close to the Lord. I certainly wasn't going to give Him my heart."

"And then . . . ?" Leslie asked softly.

"And then . . ." He gave her that same extraordinarily tender smile, and once again her head was spinning. "And then you came along. I took a lot of my anger out on you, but you kept forgiving me. You even prayed for me. And despite your . . . background, you seemed to have such an easy, loving rapport with the Lord. I was puzzled, because nothing seemed to fit. I kept thinking about the things you said, watching how you made your faith a living, *doing* thing. Finally I told the Lord that He could have *all* of my life, and my heart, too. That was when He began to show me that I would never really be fulfilled as a physician until I came back to my roots.

"And it was my heart that made me drive out here to-night, too, Leslie. You were never out of my thoughts—I missed you and wanted you—but if I had let my pride rule, instead of my heart, I would still be in Cincinnati. And none of this would have happened."

"Oh, Steven . . ." They had come so close to losing each other. If they hadn't been willing to follow the Lord's leading. . . . She didn't want to think about it.

Instead she asked another question, one that had been

nagging at her during the entire evening. "Will it be hard for you to give up the clinic administration job and . . . will you miss Rita very much?"

"Rita?" He looked blank. "Why would I miss Rita? Oh, we dated when I moved there, but it was never serious, not on my part, at any rate. Her goals and interests are a lot different than mine, although I guess her lifestyle seemed attractive for a while. Come to think of it, she did seem upset when I turned down the clinic offer."

Leslie could certainly see why. Honestly, men could be so naive sometimes. "But I thought her father and the board had certain conditions."

"They did. No abortions at the clinic, and the administrator had to live in Cincinnati. At that point I had already decided to move here. The man they chose was recommended by me; that's why the banquet was such a good night for all of us. The whole project was finally launched, and the right man was at the helm. I have agreed to do some outpatient surgery there a few days each month."

"But, Steven . . ." Leslie's head was getting fuzzy again. "I . . . I thought . . . weren't you with Rita at the banquet?"

"No, I came alone. I hadn't dated Rita in ages. Where did you get that idea?"

"Oh, just a silly notion." Women could be naive, too, she reflected. From now on, she would *ask* Steven instead of believing the rumors that would probably always circulate around handsome and appealing men.

"Any more questions?" Steven drew her gently toward him.

"No." She drank in the sight of him and knew that she would never tire of being a part of him, a part of the new life he was beginning. Kentucky, the land where they would live, not only tomorrow, but hopefully, for a lifetime. *Oh, Lord, thank you, thank you. . . .*

Steven was just starting to kiss her when Dotty appeared in the doorway, flushed and excited. "Dr. Steve! Leslie! You've got to come. Margaret is in labor!"

Creation. God's cycle continuing. And they would be a part of it. "Let's go and bring that baby into the world, love," Steven said, pulling Leslie to her feet. "And then let's buy a ring and plan a wedding."

Teen Series From
Bethany House Publishers

Early Teen Fiction (11–14)

HIGH HURDLES by Lauraine Snelling
Show jumper DJ Randall strives to defy the odds and achieve her dream of winning Olympic Gold.

SUMMERHILL SECRETS by Beverly Lewis
Fun-loving Merry Hanson encounters mystery and excitement in Pennsylvania's Amish country.

THE TIME NAVIGATORS by Gilbert Morris
Travel back in time with Danny and Dixie as they explore unforgettable moments in history.

Young Adult Fiction (12 and up)

CEDAR RIVER DAYDREAMS by Judy Baer
Experience the challenges and excitement of high school life with Lexi Leighton and her friends—over one million books sold!

GOLDEN FILLY SERIES by Lauraine Snelling
Readers are in for an exhilarating ride as Tricia Evanston races to become the first female jockey to win the sought-after Triple Crown.

JENNIE MCGRADY MYSTERIES by Patricia Rushford
A contemporary Nancy Drew, Jennie McGrady's sleuthing talents promise to keep readers on the edge of their seats.

LIVE! FROM BRENTWOOD HIGH by Judy Baer
When eight teenagers invade the newsroom, the result is an action-packed teen-run news show exploring the love, laughter, and tears of high school life.

THE SPECTRUM CHRONICLES by Thomas Locke
Adventure and romance await readers in this fantasy series set in another place and time.

SPRINGSONG BOOKS by various authors
Compelling love stories and contemporary themes promise to capture the hearts of readers.

WHITE DOVE ROMANCES by Yvonne Lehman
Romance, suspense, and fast-paced action for teens committed to finding pure love.